# fire & ice

## ROBBI RENEE

LOVE NOTES BY ROBBI RENEE

# *synopsis*

Welcome to Seduction in Red, White, and Blue — a sultry singles retreat for the grown and unapologetically sexy on the shores of Bimini.

For Blaize Raymond and Icelyn Perry, the attraction is immediate... and dangerously familiar.

Once, theirs was a May–December flame — she, the seasoned storm, he, the younger spark. What started as heat turned into something neither was ready to claim.

Now the years have shifted the balance. He's grown. Grounded. Intentional. And the chemistry between them? Still electric.

Under fireworks and moonlit skies, Fire and Ice collide again — not reckless but refined. Not fleeting, but inevitable.

Because some connections don't fade with time.

They burn hotter.

# blaize

"Hi, Mom," Blyss said, casually. Almost too casually as if she knew her mom was about to be on her usual bullshit.

"Hey, babygirl," Alyssa replied, her voice bubbling with affection. "I can't wait to see you."

"I can't wait to see you, too." Blyss smiled, but her eyes snapped back to the soccer game on the big screen, thumbs flying over the controller.

"Bumblebee, why are you answering my phone?" I asked, stepping into the room that used to be my man cave that was now overtaken by soccer balls and bracelet making kits.

"It's Mom, Daddy," she said without even glancing at me.

*Ah, here we go.* I shook my head and grabbed the phone from the table, giving her a gentle nudge on the shoulder before collapsing onto the couch beside her. Sweat clung to my brow after a brutal workout, and I took a breath to settle myself. It was the first day of summer break, and clearly, my rising sixth grader had already checked out of reality and into Xbox FC.

"Hey," I muttered, not realizing it was a video call until Alyssa's face filled the screen.

"Hey," she echoed, flashing a smile that landed somewhere between sweet and too damn flirtatious.

I sighed and tugged a shirt over my head, resisting the urge to roll my eyes.

"Don't be shy, Blaize. I've seen all of you, babe," she teased with a giggle.

And there it was; the line Alyssa never failed to toe. I think I did rolled my eyes that time. Don't get me wrong, she was still gorgeous—hazel eyes, flawless skin, that smile that used to weaken me. *Used to.* Now, it just reminded me of the mess I'd spent years untangling.

"Yeah, well, I'm not putting on a show today," I said flatly, keeping my tone neutral for Blyss's sake. The last thing my daughter needed was a front-row seat to her parents' unresolved drama.

Alyssa's smile lingered on the screen a beat too long, as if she still thought charm could erase history. I shook my head. She was my ex for a reason. Her beauty might've been blinding once, but it couldn't hide her selfish ass fuck ways. Selfish didn't even scratch the surface when it came to Alyssa.

Even after six years of being divorced, my ex still shot her shot from time to time. And I turned her down every single time. Hard to believe that one barbecue would kick off a chain of events that led to a baby, a marriage, a divorce, and full-time fatherhood.

I met Alyssa Weathers at a retirement party in Chicago for one of my dad's Navy buddies, Colonel Hamilton Weathers. My mom was too sick to travel from St. Louis, and my sister was on bed rest with a complicated pregnancy, so I stepped in as my dad's wingman.

My father, Captain Thomas Raymond, couldn't drive after dark anymore. Cataracts had wrecked his night vision, so I took the five-hour drive off his plate and turned it into a guys' weekend. Chicago was beautiful that summer, and we made the most of it.

The party was a classic old-school kick back. A house in the suburbs, lawn chairs on the grass, and meat smoked down to the bone. Friends, family, veterans from every rank passed stories around right along with the potato salad.

I was standing off to the side, beer in hand, watching my dad hold court when I saw *her*. She stood near the covered patio, mid-laugh with a small circle of women, light brown hair brushing against caramel skin that seemed to catch every flicker of sunlight. There was a glow about her. Something that made you pause without knowing why. Her body didn't just hint at time spent in the gym; it flaunted it. And that dress? It clung in all the right ways, framing an ass that refused to be ignored.

I damn sure couldn't stop staring. My dick responded before I could talk myself down. But I held the line. I had my fill of casual flings—enough to know how easily they could blur the line between fun and fallout. The last one almost did, and I wasn't trying to bleed from that wound again.

At almost thirty, I was done with fast and fleeting. I wanted something real. Something that lasted past sex and sunrise. But the woman across the yard had other plans. We traded stares like we'd already fucked and were just basking in the sweaty afterglow.

My grin widened when hers curled back, wicked and suggestive. Every time I tried to look away, I felt her gaze trace me from the locs pulled back at my neck to the fresh J's on my feet. She bit her bottom lip, tilted her head, then gave a slow nod before stepping away from her group. The unspoken invitation was obvious to no one but me.

I had no business following this woman. None whatsoever. But the sight of that ass jiggling was like watching a flame catch silk. Beautiful, dangerous, and instantaneous. A spark that turned into fire before I even realized I was burning. She was like the first hit of good dope, and I was a damn fiend before I even had a taste.

This random beauty was the kind of high I couldn't walk away from, and I was already chasing the rush. She shot me a look over her shoulder, one that didn't ask, but dared me to *fuck around and find out.*

I glanced at my pops, who was too busy yelling, "This motherfucker right here—" mid-story, to notice me slipping away. I followed her like a puppy, hips, ass, and audacity leading the way. She didn't rush. Didn't stumble. Just moved like temptation through the kitchen, up the backstairs, into a bedroom like she owned it. Every few steps, she glanced back, teasing and testing me. As if I wasn't already possessed.

We dipped into the first bedroom. I took a second to scan the space. It was neat and cozy with a queen-sized poster bed taking up most of the room with a lounge chair by the window and plain dresser against the wall.

Random Beauty stood by the window, silhouetted by the setting sun. Damn, she was fine. White-painted toes, silver strappy sandals winding halfway up her calves, and a white mini dress clinging to curves that looked hand-sculpted. She leaned against the dresser, tipped her cup back, and looked at me over the rim. I wasn't a small nigga so her perusal of me took a minute. Her eyes scanned my bulky frame and bowed legs like we had history. We didn't. But maybe we were about to make it.

"You are so damn sexy," she said finally.

And that was all it took. I don't know who moved first, and I didn't care. In seconds, we were tangled—kissing, grabbing, biting—like our bodies had already made the decision. She yanked my shorts and boxers down to free my dick like we were long-lost lovers catching up on missed time.

Dropping to a squat, I watched her ass pop out of the tiny dress. But it was the way those pretty eyes glanced up to greet mine that had me under her spell. They lingered with her lashes lowered just enough to suggest a little restraint, but then they lifted on me with sexy confidence. Random Beauty tongued the tip of me and wasted no time swallowing me whole.

"Goddamn, ma."

The grunt tore out of me, deep and guttural, because this woman was sucking me like she'd missed me. Like I was the best thing she'd ever tasted. I was close to busting, but I couldn't go out like this. Not when I needed to feel that pussy she'd been flaunting all night.

I yanked her face, firm enough to get my dick out of her mouth, but gentle enough to let her know I wanted more. She stood up, licking her lips like she wanted more, too. I lifted her, nudging thick legs to lock around my waist. Our kisses were hot and reckless. Tongues wound together, disorderly and messy in the best way.

My back hit the wall as I slid into her. It was raw, rampant, no hesitation, no protection. She circled on me like she knew me. Like this wasn't our first time. Like we didn't care that fifty people were downstairs doing the electric slide.

We moved in sync—loud and wild as the rhythm of the party matched our own. I gripped her ass, slamming her onto me like I needed it to survive. Her arms clung around my neck, her moans pushing me closer to the edge.

"Fuck me harder," she begged, and I damn sure obliged.

Her mouth found my neck, licking, sucking, leaving marks I wouldn't bother explaining.

"Damn," she cried out, voice trembling. "Damn," she gasped again, more strained this time as if my mans was hitting her throat.

The crash of our orgasms wasn't pretty. It was frenzied, uncontrolled, and unexpectantly real. The kind of beautiful that only existed in chaos. I pulled out faster than my dick desired, praying I'd timed it right. But before I could catch my breath, she slid her slick heat along my length again, coaxing me back to life.

The only thing that slowed us down was the phone she'd tossed on the bed when we walked in. It rang once, then twice. She broke away from with a breathless laugh.

"Damn, baby," she said to me before answering the phone.

I slipped into the bathroom to clean up because I needed to get the hell away from Random Beauty. After her voice stopped, I expected her to join me but she didn't. I waited a minute, then another, then the door clicked. She was gone.

I washed up, splashed water on my face, and stared at myself in the mirror - still half hard and fully embarrassed. The high was gone. In its place: regret I couldn't name but could definitely feel. I'd smashed a woman I didn't know at a retirement party. For one of my dad's friends, no less.

When I stepped back into the party, it was like she never existed. No trace. No name. No nothing. Later that night, while my dad was still holding court with Colonel Weathers, I spotted her again, moving through the crowd like I hadn't had her pressed against a bedroom wall an hour ago. She didn't even look my way.

"Blaize, I want you to meet my daughter, Lieutenant Alyssa Weathers," Colonel Weathers said, pride thick in his voice as he kissed her forehead. Alyssa and I exchanged a tight, uneasy smile. "My baby girl's headed to San Diego next week. Just got accepted into the Navy Nurse Corps," he added with a wide grin.

*Shit.*

That night was the last time I saw Alyssa. There was no way in hell I'd knowingly slept—correction, *fucked*—with my father's friend's daughter. Especially not a Navy officer. And definitely not one who'd be living across the country by the time the weekend was over.

I figured that was the end of it. One wild night, no strings. Until seven months later, the past came crashing back. Imagine my disbelief when my father called me completely frantic.

*"Colonel just called me. His daughter is in labor. She's in San Diego. Said you need to get there right away. Blaize... what the hell did you do, son?"*

"Blaize, what time does her flight get in?" Alyssa asked, snapping me out of the memory like cold water to the face.

I blinked. "I'm sorry, what? Her flight?"

She nodded, calm as ever, like what she said made any damn sense. I scoffed and shook my head. This woman was unbelievable. Blyss shot me a glance from the couch, then quickly turned her eyes back to the big screen, but I knew she was listening. She always listened, even when she pretended not to.

I held up a finger. "Hold on," I ordered, stepping out of the room.

No way was my daughter about to sit through another episode of her parents falling apart in real time. Closing the double doors to the media room, I made my way downstairs. Alyssa stayed on the screen, watching me without saying a word.

Once in my bedroom, I shut the door, then stepped into the bathroom and closed that door, too. I needed two sets of doors between me and the rage simmering in my chest. If she was flaking on Blyss again, I was about to let her have it.

"Alyssa," I said, voice low and clipped, "...our daughter doesn't have a flight. You're supposed to fly to Chicago to pick her up from your parents after her visit with them. That was the plan."

"Blaize," she sighed, dragging out my name like I was the one being difficult. "I thought I told you my plans changed."

I bit my bottom lip hard enough to hurt. "Nah. You didn't."

I stared into the phone. If I could've reached through it, I would've. This was classic Alyssa—set an expectation, then twist it last-minute without warning. And somehow I was always the bad guy for holding her accountable for her unmotherly actions.

"I'm not going to be able to do that," she said, eyes shifting to the side like she couldn't even lie directly to my face.

"Then you won't be able to see Blyss," I said flatly, gripping the edge of the bathroom sink. "You do this every fucking time, Alyssa. Damn." My voice cracked a little, louder than I meant.

I took a breath, remembering my daughter was still upstairs. "She's packed. She's excited. And now you want me to pick up the pieces. Again."

"It's not like that, B. Blyss is still coming. I just need her to fly directly here."

"To Hawaii?" I snapped, stepping toward the screen. "You want our ten-year-old daughter to fly from Chicago to Hawaii by herself for eight, maybe nine hours? Are you insane?" I dragged a hand down my face, trying to push the disbelief out through my skin.

"This cannot be my life," I whispered.

The way Alyssa and I met should've told me everything I needed to know about how unpredictable things with her would always be.

"She's flown alone before," she said, like that somehow justified this mess.

"Yeah. From St. Louis to Chicago. One hour, tops. Not halfway across the damn world."

"Okay, okay, I get it," she muttered, throwing her hands up. "You don't want me to spend time with my daughter."

"Don't do that, Alyssa." I warned, locking eyes with the screen. "We made a plan. Every single time, you change it to work for you. You don't stop to think about how it affects your daughter or me."

Alyssa Nichelle Weathers always knew how to make an entrance and an impact. But I was done letting her make a mess. My voice was tight yet controlled. Just above a whisper now, but every syllable was heavy.

"I've worked too hard to be the parent who stays calm, who shows up, who shields our daughter from this kind of chaos. I'm not letting you unravel that because you feel like changing plans last minute." I started pacing the bathroom, clenching and unclenching my fists, holding it together for my Bumblebee. Shit, one of us had to.

"Yo ass is selfish, man. When are you gonna think about somebody other than yourself?"

Alyssa's voice faded into background noise as I thought about everything that led us here. After my father hit me with the news that my one-night stand was pregnant and claiming I was the father, I sat in my car in the cold of February for two hours, trying to figure out what the hell I was supposed to do.

The math added up. It could be my baby. But if she was the kind of woman who'd sleep with a dude without knowing his name, could she also be the type to lie about who the father was? And she was delivering early. Way too early. Still, I knew if something happened to the baby and I hadn't shown up, I'd regret it for the rest of my life.

*Me? A father? Fuck.*

I booked a red-eye to California with no clue where I'd stay. I just knew I had to get there. After a tense call with Alyssa's father, Colonel Weathers gave me the full story. Alyssa had hidden the pregnancy. Her parents didn't even know until a nurse from the military hospital called to say she was in labor - at just 29 weeks. My background as an EMS and nursing school told me that it was serious.

By the time I stepped onto the labor and delivery floor at Naval Medical Center San Diego, it was just after six in the morning. I was exhausted and completely unprepared, but my gut told me the truth... I needed to be there.

The nurse pointed to the waiting area where her family sat. Faces I recognized from the backyard barbecue turned to look at me; some confused, some full of quiet judgment.

Colonel Weathers stood and placed a steady hand on my shoulder before leading me to Alyssa's room. She was asleep when we walked in, but her eyes fluttered open. Her gaze landed on her father first, then widened when they met mine.

"Blaize." Hearing her say my name for the first time, especially under these circumstances, hit different. "I'm so sorry," she croaked, voice raw and trembling as tears streamed down her cheeks.

I couldn't even look at her. This was a woman I'd known for maybe five hours total and now we were tied together in a way that felt terrifyingly permanent. All I could do was nod. I couldn't say a word.

But damn, even in that hospital bed, she was beautiful. Her caramel skin still glowed, her hair had grown well past her shoulders, and those hazel eyes—blurred with tears— still had a way of catching light.

"The baby?" I finally asked, the words cracked and barely audible: half-question, half-plea.

Colonel Weathers tapped my elbow, nodding for me to follow. At that point, I was just a passenger, letting him lead me through the wreckage I couldn't yet process.

My eyes locked onto the glowing letters: NICU. Neonatal Intensive Care Unit. I kept walking, but I couldn't feel my legs. It was like moving through a nightmare I couldn't wake up from. A nurse met us at the entrance and gave clear, practiced instructions: wash to the elbows, cover your head, put on the gown.

I just nodded, silent and moving on autopilot. My hands

obeyed, but my mind lagged behind. My heart pounded like a war drum in my chest as I prepared to meet a child whose future was uncertain.

The nurse guided me into a dim room where an incubator glowed softly. Tubes, monitors, beeps—every sound and wire added weight to the moment. Then I saw her. She was so small, wrapped in machines and wires. Her eyes were covered with white tape, feet swallowed by socks that didn't fit, her head no bigger than my palm under a tiny hat.

But her skin was smooth and cinnamon brown, just like mine. Her little fingers twitched and lips puckered softly. And in that instant, I felt something shift inside me. A nurse placed a gentle hand on my back.

"It looks worse than it is, Dad," she said. "We take every precaution with these little ones. But she's strong. She's a fighter. And look at that little smile. She's a delight."

I nodded, but the weight of it all hit me at once and the tears followed. I didn't know if that baby was mine. But I wanted her to be. God, I wanted her to be mine.

Three days later, the test confirmed what my heart already knew: 99.99% chancc I was hcr father. Blyss Mirielle Raymond came into this world at barely three pounds, fighting but fierce. Even surrounded by the hiss of machines and blinking lights, she was pure light herself. That's why I named her *Blyss Mirielle*, because even in the chaos and confusion, she was my joyful miracle. My reason to breathe different. To do better.

"Blaize, just hear me out. She's a big gir—" Alyssa's

annoying voice broke through my reverie like shattered glass.

I cut her off before she could finish that stupid-ass sentence. "Nope. My daughter is not flying that long by herself. You either figure out how to get to Chicago like we planned, or Blyss stays with your parents and comes back home after. And forget Christmas, because that shit won't be happening either."

Alyssa went silent. The only thing I heard was the occasional sniffle. "I love my daughter, Blaize," she said softly.

I pressed my lips together and shook my head, trying to keep from saying what I really wanted to say. I didn't doubt that Alyssa loved Blyss. Our daughter was our pride and joy, but love didn't cancel out *selfishness*. Alyssa had always struggled to put anyone's needs above her own, even our daughter's.

For months, I flew back and forth between St. Louis and California, juggling work, fatherhood, and the guilt of missing moments I could never get back. During that time, Alyssa and I got... friendly again. Too friendly. Those late-night calls that were supposed to be about the baby turned into conversations about everything else. And before long, they turned into visits that had nothing to do with parenting.

Eventually, that blurred line led me to pack up my life in Missouri and move to California. Being near my daughter made the move worth it. Especially with the medical complications she had early on from being born premature. I missed my family. I missed my roots. But nothing compared to watching your child grow up in real time.

As Alyssa and I learned to co-parent, we started to find a rhythm. Somewhere in that fragile groove, we convinced ourselves it was more than it was. On impulse, we got married at the courthouse. Just us, baby Blyss, and two of Alyssa's military friends as witnesses.

I told myself it was the right thing to do. Both of our parents had been married for decades. We knew what lasting love looked like and thought we could replicate it.

But that wasn't our story.

Not even two years in, Alyssa's selfishness began to unravel everything. Every decision had to suit her: her schedule, her needs, her comfort. She rarely stopped to consider how her choices affected the people around her… including our daughter.

"I know you do, Alyssa," I said, voice strained. "But everything can't revolve around you. Every plan, every decision… it can't all be based on what works for *you*. Blyss comes first. Always."

I let that sit. She swiped at her tears and turned her face slightly from the screen. I knew she was tired of hearing this, but I'd say it again and again if I had to. Especially when it came to our daughter. Alyssa's broken promises might not mean much to her now, but one day they'd add up and Blyss would feel every crack.

"You can't keep brushing off her feelings and expect me to patch up the pieces. She deserves better… from the both of us."

Alyssa nodded, tears slipping freely down her cheeks now. "I'll move some things around... try to get there a few days early," she murmured. "Tell babygirl I'll call her tomorrow."

I nodded, though I was already done with the conversation. I'd had to check her too many times, and I knew this wouldn't be the last.

"Bye," she said, barely above a whisper.

I nodded once more and ended the call without a goodbye. Letting the phone rest against my forehead, I gritted my teeth and let out a low, silent groan. My body's way of releasing what my mouth couldn't. The moment barely settled before I heard a soft knock at the door.

"Daddy?" Blyss said gently, nudging the door open.

I jumped, nearly slipping off the edge of the bathtub where I'd been sitting, elbows on my knees, lost in my own head.

"Yeah, Bee. Come in, babygirl," I said, straightening up.

A pair of hazel eyes, just like her mother's, met mine. People always said Blyss was my twin, but that's only because they rarely saw Alyssa. The truth was, she carried both of us. With her crown of sandy-brown coils pulled into a high ponytail, floral-print glasses perched on her round nose, and that always-observant gaze, she looked every bit the thoughtful, curious girl I was raising... and maybe even a little worried.

I gave her a soft nod, motioning for her to sit next to me. Before she could even open her mouth, I cut off whatever doubt was circling in that beautiful mind of hers.

"Mom's coming a day or two before your trip. She said she'll call you tomorrow so you two can plan all the fun stuff," I said, giving her a quick tickle to lighten the mood.

A smirk tugged at the corner of her lips. "I can stay with Gammy and PeePop if you wanna go on your trip, Daddy," she offered, trying to sound casual. "It's not a big deal. I want you to have fun for your birthday."

I wrapped an arm around her. "You're hanging with your grandparents like we planned. Then it's time with your mom. You two always have fun, right?"

She shrugged, nodding slowly.

"Right," I said, tickling her side again.

This time, she squirmed and broke into a fit of giggles. "Right, Daddy. Right!" she squealed.

"Now come on," I said, ruffling her ponytail and pulling her in close, "so I can go ahead and whoop you on this game."

*blaize*

"Damn, dawg. That's drink number two and we haven't been here an hour," my friend, Jordan, exclaimed.

I eyed him while guzzling down the final sip of cognac.

"Where is my God-daughter tonight? Do I need to pick her up?" Jordan's tone was teasing but he did not play about Blyss.

Jordan Charles and I had been friends since the eighth grade. We were more like brothers than friends. His family moved next door to us, and one day after school, we bonded over football and girls with big booties.

"Alyssa was on her bullshit again today."

"Don't tell me she canceled," Jordan exclaimed, knowing the games my ex-wife played.

I shook my head. "Nah. She tried to change the plan but

didn't tell anybody but her damn self. I got it straight though," I said, summoning the waitress for another drink.

"Damn, man. Save all that drinking for the all-inclusive vacation that starts in -", Jordan's voice trailed off as he glanced at his watch, "- eleven days," he bantered.

I channeled my pre-teen daughter and rolled my eyes. While I desperately needed a vacation, I was not looking forward to this particular one. My adventurous best friend decided that we should go on a trip for singles forty and older in Bimini.

Twenty strangers; ten men and ten women, living in a mansion on the beach for five days over the extended fourth of July weekend sounded like some reality TV shit to me.

"Man, this shit is about to be an orgy for old folks," I laughed.

"Nigga, speak for yourself. I may be forty but this dick ain't old," Jordan quipped.

"Don't ever talk to me about your raggedy ass dick, *ever again*," I snickered, shaking my head at this dude.

"Nah, but fa'real. I think it's going to be a good time. My homegirl, Sienna, started organizing these trips for her friends just for fun, but when people offered to pay her, she left her job and became an entrepreneur."

"Your homegirl, huh?" I asked, questioningly.

Jordan wasn't the type of dude to have female friends without extra benefits.

He nodded. "Just my homegirl." Jordan lifted a brow. "Don't get me wrong, she's fine and cool as hell, but Sienna is likely more your speed."

"Why you say that?" I lifted a curious brow.

"Because she's um... seasoned," Jordan chuckled.

"Seasoned. What is she... A steak?" I furrowed my brow.

"You know what I mean, man. I think Deon Cole called women of a certain age... *vintage*," Jordan explained.

I stared at him like he was an idiot. "So now she's a piece of furniture."

"Nigga, she's older, shit," Jordan declared frustratingly.

"Like how old?" I questioned.

"Sienna is probably forty-eight, forty-nine." He shrugged dismissively.

"Dude... you're forty. Eight years older makes her *old*," I probed, motioning air quotes.

"For the record, I did not say old. I said seasoned... vintage. You know, she's auntie status," Jordan snickered.

"And nigga, you're *uncle* status to these young ass girls you deal with," I laughed. "Don't knock it until you try it, though," I continued. "A woman who knows what the hell she wants and ain't afraid to tell you is sexy. I like a woman who'll grab my head while my tongue is in that shit and direct me where she wants me to go. That shit turns me on," I smiled, making eye contact with a woman across the bar that fit my description perfectly.

I nodded then raised my drink in recognition. She returned the sentiment.

Jordan rolled his eyes. "Man, I don't want a controlling woman who tries to treat me like a lil ass boy," Jordan scoffed. "Those *I don't need a man* type women. No thank you."

"You do realize that this trip is for people forty *and over*, right?" I stressed.

Jordan nodded. "I know. I know. Let's just say I am ready to try something new."

"Like Sienna," I teased and Jordan lifted a brow. Chuckling, I asked, "What's the name of her company again?"

"Soul Quest Adventures," he answered.

"Hmmm. Well let the *adventure* begin," I said, tapping my beer bottle against Jordan's glass.

# FOUR

# Jocelyn

"Bryson Perry Williams, Jr., Bachelor of Mechanical Engineering, *summa cum laude*," the dean called out as my baby boy walked across the stage.

A sea of our family and friends erupted in screams, completely ignoring the request to hold applause. But let's be honest, did they really think Black folks were gonna wait until *all* the names were called? We worked too damn hard for that kind of silence.

"That's my baby!" I hollered, holding up the oversized poster with Bryson's handsome face.

Not only was I one proud mama, I was also a newly minted empty nester. My oldest daughter, Kamryn, had flown the nest nearly two years ago after finishing her master's degree, and now Bryson was packed and preparing to head to Atlanta for his new job in a couple of months. I couldn't decide if I was ecstatic about it or sad as hell.

"And that's my son!" Bryson's father shouted from the other end of the row, disrupting my thoughts.

My squinted eyes darted down the aisle of family members and landed on Bryson Williams, Sr., the father of my children and sometimes, the bane of my existence. His hazelnut skin and big honey-brown eyes—the same ones he'd given my kids—were beaming with pride. I rolled my eyes, because he was still as fine as he'd been twenty years ago.

As much as he grinded every last one of my nerves and our relationship had been one of those shoot-straight-up-then-plummet-to-the-ground kind of rollercoasters, I had to admit: he was an outstanding dad and my favorite frenemy.

Bryson Sr.—though I'd always called him Sonny—and I had known each other practically since birth. Our single mothers moved into the same apartment building when we were just a few months old, and once they became friends, the rest was history. From the stroller to the school bus, Sonny and I were a package deal. Practically glued at the hip and impossible to separate.

Most people assumed we were like siblings because of how close our mothers were. But truthfully? I had a crush on him since I knew what a crush was. By freshman year, his behavior toward me had shifted from "play cousin" to something else and it was game over. He'd always been so dang cute, with those tell-all eyes, a soft carpet of curly hair, and a chunky frame that transformed into a thickset build by high school.

Much to our mothers' delight, we started dating sophomore year. They were already planning the wedding, picking baby names, and mapping out the house with the white picket fence by the time we were set to graduate. *Hell, I guess I had those same dreams, too.*

I snickered, remembering how I used to write *Mrs. Williams* in big, loopy letters all over my notebooks. I even signed everybody's senior yearbook as *Mrs. Icelyn Camille Williams.* And yet, here I am—twenty-something years later —still *Miss* Icelyn *Perry.*

I was sure that when Sonny left for the Air Force after high school, he'd come back for me. That he'd make me his wife. His promises of a future together were enough for me to believe in, even when life took unexpected turns.

By twenty-one, in my junior year of college, I was pregnant with our daughter. I dropped out to have her and less than two years later, I was pregnant again. He proposed, and for a while, I thought we were building something solid. But by the time our kids were seven and five, I knew there was no real future for us as a couple.

Sonny and I could finish each other's sentences. We knew each other better than anyone else. But we could never make it work. We fought like cats and dogs but made love like lions — fierce, hungry, and unwilling to let go. He proposed, then pulled back. I tried to move on, but he had a way of drawing me back with the same passion and promises that had hooked me from the start.

Over time, that passion fizzled, replaced by frustration and resentment. We finally agreed on one thing—we were better partners in parenting than in life together.

"Congratulations, Lyn," Sonny said, pulling me into a hug.

The group of almost twenty family members was standing in front of the stadium, waiting for Bryson Jr. to emerge.

"Congrats to you too, Sonny. We did a good job."

He nodded, swiping at a tear. "Yeah. Yeah, we did."

I shook my head. "You've always been such a punk," I teased, nudging his arm.

He chuckled because he knew I was right. Especially when it came to our kids. This man cried at every milestone like it was the series finale of his favorite show.

"Ma!" I heard my son's voice slice through the crowd.

"BJ!" I squealed as he wrapped me in a giant hug.

Burying his face into my shoulder, my baby boy sobbed tears of joy, and probably a little exhaustion. School had never come easy for Bryson. Years of speech therapy, reading specialists, tutors, and pure grit brought him to this moment. He refused to fail, and today was proof that he'd won. He pulled his dad into a hug next, and the waterworks kept flowing.

"I'm so proud of you, son. So damn proud," Sonny choked out.

"B-boy!" my daughter Kamryn sang, doing a goofy little shimmy as she weaved through the sea of people.

Bryson lifted his head, still grinning through tears. That smile—the one that could light up a whole room—spread across his face the moment he spotted his sister. His favorite person in the world, second only to me.

He danced toward her, mirroring her moves until they collapsed into each other's arms.

"You did it, B. You *did* it," she squealed, cupping his face in her hands.

They were thick as thieves, those two. Always had been. And Sonny and I wouldn't have it any other way.

---

OVER FIFTY PEOPLE traipsed throughout my house and backyard for Bryson's graduation party and my *tired* was tired. I didn't want to see another line dance or hear any more fans clapping for at least a month.

I stood at the kitchen sink, elbow-deep in soapy water, washing the last round of dishes while Bryson and his dad gathered up the trash.

"Where's your daughter?" I asked Sonny.

He chuckled. "Uh oh... she's *my* daughter now? That means she's pissed you off."

"Yeah, she is. Because I told her she was on kitchen duty with me," I fussed.

"She's outside with David," Bryson muttered, his face tight with a scowl.

My eyes locked with Sonny's, and just like that, we were on the same page. Concern, frustration, and a shared dislike we didn't even have to speak aloud.

David was our daughter Kam's fiancé. The one *nobody* liked. He proposed on her birthday a few months ago, and now he was moving in with her. I hadn't trusted him since he first showed up two years ago. Something about him never sat right in my spirit. His skinny, high-yella ass was smooth. Too smooth and too calculated.

And lately, his need for control wasn't subtle anymore. I saw it in my daughter's posture. The way her shoulders curved inward like she was shrinking. I heard it in her voice. In the pauses where confidence used to live.

Kamryn used to be fire. Now, sometimes, she barely sparked. But she was grown, so all I could do was pray, stay close, and be ready when the pieces started falling.

"Hey, y'all," Kamryn called as she walked in, her pretty face mirroring mine.

My smile was automatic... until David walked in behind her.

"Kamryn, I told you I needed help in the kitchen," I said, already hearing the edge creep into my voice.

"Well, here I am," she replied, just a little too sharp. "What do you need me to do?"

I looked around at the counters covered in foil pans, the red cups scattered everywhere, and she had the nerve to ask me *what needed to be done*?

"Girl—" I started, but her father cut in before I took it there.

"Kamryn—" he said, calm but firm, "you see what needs to be done. Just jump in and help." Then he turned to David. "You can help us get the rest of this trash out."

David gave a weak smile and pointed toward the door behind him.

"Oh, uh, Bryson, I gotta—" he said smugly.

"Mr. Williams," Sonny said, gritting through clenched teeth.

"Um, Mr. Williams, I gotta head out," David continued.

Sonny shook his head. "Of course you do, David," he muttered.

"Y'all have a good night," David said. "KK, walk me to the car."

Three sets of eyes snapped in his direction so fast, it might've created wind. His tone was always curt and demanding. The whole family had been biting our tongues for Kamryn's sake, but this lil' knucklehead-ass nigga was working *every* last iota of patience I had.

"If y'all walking to the car, y'all can take some trash," Bryson Jr. said, shifting his eyes from them to the row of trash bags.

Sonny and I locked eyes again, both of us fighting the urge to laugh. BJ was *very* protective of his big sister, almost more than me and his father. I stayed quiet and kept wiping down the counters and packing up the leftover food while I watched BJ, Kam, and David carry the trash out to the garage.

"I don't know how much more I can take," I whispered to Sonny.

He nodded, releasing an exasperated breath.

"That lil mutherfucka gonna make me go to jail," he said, leaning against the counter, taking another swig of beer.

"I got some bail money set aside for you," I chuckled and he snickered.

The silent reprieve was only momentary when we heard raised voices coming back through the garage.

"You know, y'all don't have to act like that with him," Kamryn said, stepping into the kitchen with her arms folded, eyes bouncing from her brother to her father... then landing on me.

I tilted my head, one brow lifted as I leaned a hip against the counter.

"Act like *what*, Kamryn?" I said, calmly drying my hands on a towel. "You mean act like *him*? Sitting in the corner all night, barely speaking to anybody? You expect us to roll out a red carpet for someone who won't even *try* to connect with your family?"

Kamryn rolled her eyes.

"Roll 'em if you want to, Kamryn Camille. I'm not here to coddle you. I'm speaking the truth. Talking to you woman to woman."

"The truth? What truth, Mama?" she snapped.

"That boy is not good for you, babygirl," her father said, stepping in.

"He sits around like he's God's gift or some shit. We're movin' tables, takin' out trash, and he's posted up like he can't break a nail. You're running back and forth, fixing his plate, bringin' him drinks, while he acts like you owe him something," Sonny said, an obvious pained expression on his face.

"Daddy, Ms. Darla fixed your plate. So what's the big deal?" Kamryn shot back, her voice tight, eyes glassy.

"The big damn deal is I've *earned* that shit," Sonny

barked. "I work. I pay bills. I take care of Darla. What the hell is *he* doing?"

"He's figuring it out," she said quietly, blinking away tears as she pouted like when she was a little girl.

"Yeah, well, he's figuring it out up in *your* shit," Sonny said, his tone sharp. "In *your* house. And I ain't raise my daughter to be nobody's footstool while some grown-ass man *figures it out.*"

I shook my head. This argument had been playing on repeat since the damn proposal. David was always *between jobs* or *figuring it out*, while my daughter—my brilliant, beautiful daughter—had a master's degree and was steadily rising in her career as a business analyst for a major company. She owned her condo, thanks to smart decisions and the downpayment Sonny and I gifted her for graduation.

Don't get me wrong, we never said David had to be highly educated. Hell, Sonny barely made it out of high school. But put anything in front of that man and he'd fix it. He earned his electrician's license and eventually started his own business from the ground up.

David? He didn't seem to want to do anything except stay up under my daughter like she was a life raft.

"Everybody calm down," I said, holding up my hand. "Can we not do this tonight?"

"I *definitely* don't want to do this tonight," Kamryn snapped, grabbing her purse from the chair and stomping toward the door.

"Camille." Sonny's bass-filled voice cut through the room like a clap of thunder.

She froze mid-step. He didn't need to say another word. When her daddy called her by her middle name, she knew what time it was. Like clockwork, she spun on her heels and walked back into the kitchen.

"Goodnight, babygirl," he said, softening as he opened his arms. "I love you."

She folded into his embrace like the spoiled daddy's girl she'd always been. He kissed her temple and leaned in, whispering something only for her.

Bryson came up beside me, resting his chin on my shoulder. We both watched the moment in silence.

"Goodnight, Ma. Have fun on your trip. I love you. And I'm sorry," Kamryn said, turning to me.

"I love you more, Kam," I said, taking a few steps toward her and pulling her in tight. Then I lowered my voice. "We're not trying to hurt you, sweetheart. We just want what's best. You know that, right?"

She nodded slowly, eyes glistening, then glanced over at Bryson. He didn't need to say a word. He slipped his arm around her shoulders and walked her to her car like it was a script they'd memorized since childhood. I let out a long exhale I hadn't realized was caught in my throat.

"She'll figure it out," I said to Sonny.

"Yeah," he whispered, eyes fixed on the now-empty doorway. "I hope so."

"Ma, I'm heading out," BJ said, poking his head into my bedroom.

I was still planted in the chair across from my bed, staring at the chaos of clothes scattered across my mattress. Looking up at him, I couldn't help but smile. My son was so damn handsome. I took him in from head to toe, grinning like a proud fool.

"You're still not packed?" he asked, chuckling.

I tilted my head and gave him my best mock-pout. "Nope. Can't seem to get it together."

"What time's your flight?" He stepped inside and sat on the edge of the bed.

"Eight. Aunt SiSi will be here by six," I groaned, glancing at the clock that had just flipped to eleven.

"Good luck, Ma," BJ laughed, crossing the room to kiss my forehead.

"Be careful, son."

"I will. I got a room downtown so I'm not driving," he informed me.

"Good. Text me when you get in." I didn't say it like a suggestion.

"Ma," he groaned.

"BJ," I mocked right back. "I know you're grown, but you're still my baby. I'm gonna worry until they toss dirt on me. Maybe even after that."

That got us both laughing.

"I love you, Ma. Be good, be careful, and have fun," he said, pulling me into a hug before heading out.

I closed my eyes and said a silent prayer for my baby boy

before turning on some music to get motivated. Packing for five days in Bimini with an unknown agenda was a challenge. To be naked or not to be naked—that was the real question.

The Peloton and Pilates had been doing this forty-eight-year-old body right, and I was tempted to flaunt it. Sure, there were still a few bumps here and a little fupa there, but I looked good and felt great.

This wasn't just a vacation; it was a reward. A celebration of my next chapter. After years of raising kids, shuttling them between school and extracurriculars, I'd finally gone back and finished my degree in marketing while they were in middle school. I'd climbed the corporate ladder, stayed twenty-one years with the same company, and now... I was stepping out on faith to start my own business.

For almost a decade, I'd been consulting as a side hustle, too afraid to make it official. When my kids were younger, I needed the security of a full-time job. But now that they were grown and gone, I could finally do something just for me.

My phone rang. No need to look because I already knew it was my best friend, Sienna. I hit my earpiece, and before I could say hello, her raspy voice filled my ear.

"Hey friend, are you packed?"

"Girl, barely. It was almost World War Three in my house tonight. I need to get focused."

"Oh Lord, what did Darla say crazy this time?" SiSi chuckled.

I laughed because Sienna knew I was always two seconds

away from getting in Sonny's girlfriend's ass. Darla and Sonny had been together almost ten years, and he seemed happy enough. She was a little awkward, but for the most part, we got along, until she started trying to parent my kids or made slick comments about me getting a man.

"Darla actually had some sense today. It was Kam who lost her whole mind about how we treat David."

"That lil' nigga gon' make me slap him about my Godchild," Sienna snapped.

I laughed again, because BJ and Sienna might be tied for how protective they were over Kamryn.

"You and me both. He's just so damn arrogant."

"Mmm-hmm, but those be the ones," she said, sipping her wine loud enough for me to hear it.

"The ones what?" I asked, moving around my room like a chicken with its head cut off.

"Now you know a broke nigga and good dick go together like trouble and tequila, chile," she laughed. "That boy probably has my niece climbing the walls."

I grimaced. "Yeah, I *do not* need nor want to hear about my daughter having sex. Especially not sex that may have her losing her damn mind."

"Well, it's probably true. But all we can do is pray. We've all had to bump our heads a time or two before we found some common sense."

She wasn't wrong, so I just nodded like she could see me. "Alright, no more talk about Kam. Tell me about this mystery trip I agreed to."

Sienna owned a travel company that curated unforgettable trips exclusively for Black travelers who wanted to connect—sometimes with a new destination, sometimes with new people. Couples' getaways, girls' trips, guys' trips, safaris, solo adventures... you name it, she could plan it.

"This one's called *Seduction in Red, White, and Blue*," she said.

"Ohhh... I need a little seduction in my life," I teased.

"Well, this trip is for the grown and sexy. All forty-plus and ready to mix and... mingle... if you know what I mean."

"So what you're telling me is to be naked and pack my best lube," I joked.

"That's exactly what I'm telling you, friend. Be ready at six and let the fireworks start poppin', baby," she cackled.

# blaize

"Are you gonna miss me, Daddy-o?" Blyss teased, shimmying her shoulders like she was on a stage.

I laughed, shaking my head at this charismatic little girl of mine. We were packing the last of her things before her flight tomorrow morning.

"Terribly, Nugget," I said, matching her shimmy with one of my own.

She giggled and just like that, I was done for. Someone may as well sprinkle fairy dust over my head, because this little girl had had me under her spell from day one. It had been that way since she crashed into my life nine weeks ahead of schedule and changed everything.

"Have you packed for your trip yet?" she asked, shoving her sketchbooks and Xbox into her overstuffed backpack.

I shook my head. "Not yet. I'm a guy. It doesn't take all

this just to go on vacation," I said, pointing at her lineup of suitcases against the wall.

"I need options," she sang, flipping her braids off her shoulder with extra flair.

I just shook my head again, smirking. My tomboy was turning into a little lady and I hated it more than I wanted to admit.

"Daddy, how long will you be gone on your trip?"

"Just a week, babygirl." I smiled, but it was half-hearted.

Truth be told, I wasn't looking forward to this trip. Jordan had been on my ass for months about it, swearing it was going to be "life-changing." I had a feeling it was more like some *Ready for Love* type setup. He kept telling me to loosen up, that I'd have a good time.

I'd just celebrated my fortieth birthday a week ago. Dinner with the family, then a quick Vegas weekend with the fellas was good enough for me. Fun, sure, but nothing wild.

Since Blyss was spending most of the summer with her grandparents, and then her mom, I figured I might as well take a real vacation. Still, for the money we shelled out for this trip? The shit better be worth it. I'm talking no strings attached... except maybe a G-string. This trip was for the forty-and-up crowd, so I hoped I'd be stepping into my forties with a bang.

---

By the time I settled into my seat on the plane, Jordan was

already two mini bottles of Jack deep and grinning like the cat that caught the canary.

"Alright, man," I said, buckling in. "You've been dodging my questions for weeks. What the hell did you sign me up for?"

He leaned back, smirked, and lowered his voice like we were about to swap state secrets.

"Two adjoining mansions. Right on the beach. Twenty people: ten men, ten women. All single…. And ready for whatever."

I blinked at him. "That's the details you just now decided to mention?"

He shrugged, sipping his drink. "Didn't want you over-thinking shit."

I gave him a look. "Translation… you knew I'd back out."

Jordan chuckled, nodding. "Exactly. But trust me, this is gonna be the best week you've had in a long time. Sunrise swims, private chefs, themed nights, the works. And yeah… the women? Let's just say they're not coming for the weather alone."

I shook my head, trying not to laugh. "Man, this sounds like some reality show shit."

"Good," he said. "Means you're finally about to start living again."

I glanced out the window as the plane taxied, thinking about the last few years. I'd been focused on raising Blyss, keeping my head down, working, and doing the responsible thing as a single father. A week in paradise with no obligations, no titles, no labels? Maybe Jordan was right. This shit could be exactly what I need.

Still, I muttered under my breath, "This trip better be worth my time."

# *icelyn*

I stepped away from the bathroom sink and turned for one last look in the full-length mirror. Smiling, I admired how my ass sat up high and round in the white bandeau dress, thanks to this new butt-lifting shaper. My knotless twists hung freely down my back, and the gold YSL heels had my calves popping. A soft, natural beat against my bronzed caramel skin was all I needed to survive this summer heat.

I was *in love* with the woman staring back at me. At forty-eight, I looked pretty damn good. Women paid good damn money for these thick lips and curvy hips. Me? I just got it from my mama.

The woman in the mirror was glowing... grounded... and just a little nervous. She was stepping into a new era with her head held high and nothing to prove. This trip was the well-deserved deep breath I needed before the whirlwind of my next obsession—Perry Consulting—took over my time, money, and energy. It was bold. Risky, even. Especially at my big age. But it was finally *my* turn.

"Knock, knock," a voice sang from the bathroom doorway.

I spun around to greet SiSi. I'd only seen her a handful of times since we landed. She'd been busy preparing the space to welcome the group tonight. We'd arrived in Bimini two days ago, and I'm so thankful I flew in early to relax and soak up this beautiful place. Oh—and help my friend, of course.

But Sienna had a highly efficient team that flawlessly executed her meticulous plans, so my ass had been sleeping in, meditating on the beach, and plunging into the pool for the past forty-eight hours like it was my full-time job.

Sienna was my "BFF" before that was even a popular term of endearment. Like my kids' father, Sienna Browning had been in my life for as long as I could remember.

Her mother was the neighborhood beautician. Every Easter, wedding, prom, and graduation, Ms. Carol had a line of women trailing in and out of her basement shop for the latest hairstyles. My mother helped manage appointments and shampoo on the weekends to earn extra money, and Sienna and I would spend all day playing with the wigs and mannequin heads.

"Damn, Lyn. You're trying to make *the men all pause,* huh?" Sienna said, snapping as she sang the last few words.

Sticking my tongue out, I shimmied my hips. But if the skin-tight blue pants and white corset top were any indication of Sienna's intentions tonight, she also came to show the hell out.

"Um, sis. You're not even here to catch a man, but all that *bait* is on full display," I teased, pointing to those triple D's spilling over.

Sienna sucked her teeth as she playfully cupped her breasts.

"Shit, I didn't bring together all these fine-ass black men just for you bitches to have all of the fun," she bantered.

"Is everything ready? Do you need any help?" I questioned.

Sienna shook her head. "We're all set up. Everyone has checked in and the party will begin shortly," she said, tossing her wavy hair over one shoulder.

"You ready?" Sienna asked, eyeing both of our reflections in the mirror as she lifted a brow.

Smiling, I nodded. "Let's get the party started."

Minutes later, I walked through the corridor to the veranda where tonight's festivities would occur. My friend really outdid herself on this trip. The two mini-mansions would be home to a group of grown and sexy singles for the next five days and four nights. The guys were in one house and the ladies were in the other; both divided by a stone-paved veranda positioned between the two homes.

The setup was definitely pulled from the pages of my favorite reality TV shows guaranteed to entice some commingling. Thankfully, there would be no cameras because I was about to cut the fuck up.

The earthy-tone stone lining the veranda looked like we

were walking the streets of Italy while luminaries brightened the path around the precisely trimmed greenery. The outdoor space was beautifully decorated in red, white, and blue. Even the pool and hot tub were illuminated in festive colors.

Glancing around, I greeted the women scattered around the patio. Everyone looked lovely in their all-white attire. Fair-skinned, dark chocolate, curvy, skinny, tall, and petite; these ladies were a gorgeous kaleidoscope of black girl magic.

*But where the hell are the men?* The growing crowd of women let me know that all of the ladies were present and accounted for, but where were the men? For a second, I thought that my best friend was playing a joke on me because not one ounce of testosterone was mixed into the crowd. The sound of the double doors creaking quickly diverted my eyes across the corridor to the guys' house.

*Damn!*

One by one, fine black men representing every size, height, and hue of the melanated spectrum strolled out of the mansion. It was *literally* raining men. Light-bright, russet-colored, and chocolate-covered, I was in heaven; like the cookie monster in an Oreo factory.

It had been far too long—eight months, to be exact, since I welcomed the warmth of a good dick into my bed. Don't get me wrong, my *bedside bae* was helping me through this drought, but there was absolutely nothing like the soft flesh of a rock-hard man splitting these folds.

I'd had my fair share of one-night stands, weekend flings,

and maintenance men but the well had run dry. The one-nighters were no longer satisfying, the weekend flings wanted more than just a weekend, and the maintenance men weren't maintaining shit.

When SiSi mentioned the idea of a grown and sexy singles trip, I was the first to sign up. Several days in paradise with endless dick options, no commitment nor expectations was my type of vacation.

"Hello. Hello. Can I have your attention please?" My friend chimed a fork against her wine glass.

The crowd hushed and turned to face her standing on the steps in front of the ladies' mansion.

"My name is Sienna Browning... but please call me SiSi. I am the Founder and CEO of Soul Quest Adventures."

I smiled proudly as clapping echoed through the air.

"Are you ready to embark on a sexy, soul-stirring adventure?" she probed, and the onlookers cheered and giggled.

"Good. Over the next few days, you'll be able to pick your own adventure. Whether you enjoy relaxing poolside, massages on the beach, or zip-lining through the woods, we've planned it all. This is a judgment-free zone for the grown and sexy, so what happens on the soul quest... stays on the soul quest."

The devious smile curving her deep red–painted lips was sneaky and salacious.

"Sexy ladies and fine-ass gents, are you ready for four nights of—" Sienna's voice trailed off dramatically. "Seduction in Red, White, and Blue?" she uttered sexily.

A lascivious body roll followed as the DJ played the

opening chords of Usher's *"Seduction."* A burst of laughter and moans roared at her silliness, and many of the women joined in with versions of their own provocative choreography.

Banter ensued as waiters carrying champagne, wine, and other libations appeared. Food stations were set up throughout the patio, and a DJ was positioned in a dark corner. After retrieving a glass of champagne, I beelined for the food. I was starving. I guess my nerves got the best of me today because I hadn't eaten since breakfast.

Piling the warm hors d'oeuvres onto my plate, I smelled the most tantalizing aroma and it wasn't the food. I was a sucker for a sultry-smelling man and immediately recognized the fresh citrus and woodsy notes. *Dior Sauvage.*

Slowly spinning on my heels, I searched for the source of the fragrance. My nose was like a hound dog on a scent. And I'd found my prey—my eyes landing on a delectable piece of dark fudge dipped in white chocolate.

The sin-scented bandit was well over six feet tall, with a low haircut and a dark beard with a hint of gray trimmed to perfection. Narrowed onyx eyes, a wide nose, and thick lips accentuated his divine face. The white linen blazer, matching pants, and white V-neck T-shirt fit his body like a glove.

*God bless the tailor. Shit, God bless his mama.* Gucci sneakers draped his feet; his only jewelry was a simple link chain and bracelet. Even the way he held the whiskey glass was sexy. Who was this... *hunk-of-a-man?*

I didn't even attempt to avert my stare. Why would I? I understood the mission for this trip: climb somebody's son nastily, unapologetically, and often. And I'd never been the type of woman to abandon a mission.

The sin-scented hunk of a man stood with another handsome guy and two women, smiling in their faces. *You better get it before I do, sis,* I thought, stuffing a crab puff into my mouth.

"Hey girl, hey," Sienna sang, quickly noticing the enchanted look on my face. "Uh oh. She sees something she likes already," she added, blushing.

"Mmhmm," I hummed, damn near moaning as I took another sip of champagne. "Hercules over there with the shiny beard," I mumbled against the rim of my glass.

A burst of laughter erupted from Sienna. "Hercules?" she said, scanning the room. Within seconds, her eyes landed on the object of my lust.

"Oh, yes, ma'am. That's Blaize, and he's a winner, baby," Sienna cackled, sticking out her tongue with a smack for good measure.

"Is that your boy he's with?" I asked, glancing at the lust-filled look on her face.

Sienna hummed. "Mm-hmm, that's Jordan's fine ass. If sexy chocolate is Hercules, then Jordan is Achilles. And I am ready for a Greek god battle."

I couldn't hold my laughter. A few sets of eyes turned our way and we quickly quieted.

"Are you sure he's forty? That baby face is too cute… and oddly familiar," I asked, still studying him with squinted eyes.

"Freshly forty, girl. Like his birthday was a few days ago

or something. So you know what that means?" SiSi asked, tracing the rim of her glass.

I shook my head, brow furrowed because I had no clue what that meant. Forking more food into my mouth, I mumbled, "What?"

"That nigga still fucking like he in his thirties," she hollered, laughing.

I coughed through a giggle. "You're awful... but I hope you're right," I said, nibbling the corner of my mouth. "Maybe he's open to a belated birthday present."

I fist-bumped SiSi as my eyes slowly traced him from the crown of his thick waves to the tip of those sparkling white sneakers.

*Hercules* must have sensed my unwavering stare, because his quick glance turned into a deliberate gaze. He surveyed me from head to toe and back up. I shifted on my heels to make sure he caught all of this goodness. Biting the corner of his lip before it curved into a smile, he lifted his glass, and I raised mine in return.

"Condoms of all sizes are available in the top drawer of your nightstand. Get yours, friend," SiSi informed, mumbling humorously as she strolled away.

"You be knowing, friend," I snickered, winking at her.

Excusing himself from the group, he closed the distance between us. I began walking away as if I hadn't seen him coming. These young girls didn't understand the game. A man loved a woman who played a little hard to get.

Placing my empty plate on the tray, I hurriedly grabbed a small bottle of water and swished it around my mouth. I didn't need traces of seaweed in my teeth while trying to flirt with this fine-ass man.

"Excuse me," his baritone boomed, sending a pulse through my kitty.

Turning slowly, I smiled with my eyes. "Yes."

"We only have a few days, so I figured we could get the formalities out of the way," he said, confidence dripping from his tone. "You are sexy as hell."

I cocked my head in mock offense, admiring him up close and trying to remember his name. I vaguely recalled Sienna telling me, but I was wed to *sin-scented Hercules* at that moment.

*Shit, seemed appropriate.* I continued to eye him intently. He was impressive from a distance, but now that we shared personal space, this man was exquisite.

"Thank you. You, on the other hand, are bold... and sexy as hell, too," I retorted, pursing my lips.

He licked his and snickered.

"You said to hell with the formalities, right?" I asked playfully.

Hercules nodded, blessing me with charming smile.

"Take a walk with me, gorgeous," he said, already extending his arm as if he knew I wouldn't decline.

I glanced at his corded arm, inked with tattoos, and whispered, "My pleasure."

# *blaize*

*Where do I know her from?* I thought, while staring at the beautiful bodacious woman wrapped in a tight-ass white dress. Every single woman out here was drop-dead gorgeous, but this chick was fascinating and somewhat familiar.

Supple caramel-colored skin glowed with a soft, inviting warmth that begged for my fingers to stroke her cheeks. Big, dark eyes and heart-shaped lips framed her pretty face. I was able to capture every detail in mere seconds.

This woman was a stallion indeed. Long, shapely legs carried her five-foot-nine-inch frame with confidence and a seductive stride. If I had to guess, she was a solid two hundred pounds.

All thighs and hips and just the right amount of breasts and ass. Her figure perfectly blends the softness and strength her bold stare exudes. She gawked at me like, *nigga if you don't get your ass over here.*

*Baddie* stared at me without flinching. And once I glanced in her direction, I stared back with unbroken focus. It was like she *willed* me to look at her, sucked in by an invisible force. After a few flirtatious moments and effortless wordplay, we decided to move our party for two to the beach just steps from the houses.

Before stepping onto the sand, I instructed her to sit down on a nearby bench to remove her shoes. Lengthy legs draped across my thighs as I unstrapped her sandals. The desire to trail my fingertips up her thighs was critical, but I snapped out of it.

There was an undeniable spark blazing between us as if our bodies were rekindling moments of the past that neither of us could recollect. Strolling down the beach, we allowed the waves to hit our bare feet. I'd been in Bimini for less than twenty-four hours and the initial regret about agreeing to this trip was swiftly fading.

Words flowed between us like the rhythmic crash and hiss of the waves' arrival and retreat. The enchanting laughter and sensual, yet innocent touching felt natural and unforced. And I didn't even know her name.

"I think I know you," I uttered.

We halted our stride just in the spot where the moon cast a silvery glow over the ocean's surface. It was surprisingly romantic, and I was oddly okay with that fact.

"What's your name, baddie?" I asked, admiring how the moon accentuated her glow.

She snickered at the moniker. "Baddie, huh?" she laughed. "I guess I can't be mad since I was calling you Hercules."

My laugh rumbled against the whisper of the waves.

"Lyn," she finally answered. "And you, *Hercules?*" she teased.

"Blaize." I said.

"Damn. That's even better than Hercules. Is that a stage name or something?" she asked with a halfway serious expression.

"Hell no," I barked through a chuckle. "Do I look like a stripper?"

Lyn shrugged. "I mean... It could be a lucrative career choice for you. I'd tuck a dollar or *twenty* in your jockstrap," she said then winked.

Instinctively, I slid my arms around her waist, filling the minuscule space between us. Our eyes locked and I don't believe either of us could explain the world of emotions hovering silently.

*Who the hell is this woman?*

The deep dimple and the tiny mole on the tip of her nose caught my attention first. Something about them tugged at me, like I'd seen them before in another lifetime. Lyn licked her lips as a loose braid slipped across her eye. I reached up, brushing it back, my hand finding the curve of her neck without me even thinking about it.

Even at her height, I was still a few inches taller, causing her to crane her neck a little to look at me. Her face was so close that our breaths mingled; the warmth tickled my nose.

Anticipation did not have time to linger with the promise of a kiss. We leaned in, noses brushing lightly before our lips met in a soft, yet eager, passionate kiss.

Lyn's fingertips crept up my chest and firmly clutched the fabric of my shirt. Any space between us dwindled to almost nothing. Our tongues harmoniously tossed and turned. She sucked my bottom lip, then my tongue, igniting something I couldn't name but had clearly felt before.

Then suddenly, an unexpected rush of nostalgia sharpened my blurred mind. Her feverish kisses, her gentle touch, and her brazen caress. *Shit,* her pussy. Every detail I buried from years ago was suddenly unearthed with vivid clarity.

Reluctantly, yet abruptly, we pulled away from the kiss at the same time. Her lips were puckered and swollen and perfect. Her pretty face, sexy body, and insatiable need were as clear as if I fucked her yesterday. Our eyes ballooned with surprise and sudden recognition.

Lyn tried to mask the spark of realization reddening her cheeks, but she *knew* who I was. And now, her identity was unmistakably clear to me.

"Madame Ice," I whispered, disbelievingly.

# *blaize & icelyn*



## ICELYN

"Lyn! Lyn!" I heard my friend, Sienna, shout.

I was in line at the concession stand when her screams startled me.

"Where's Kami's inhaler?" she yelled, running full speed toward me.

Immediately, my relaxed demeanor turned frantic. I ran toward the soccer field, passing a breathless Sienna.

"She can't breathe. She can't breathe," SiSi huffed, trailing behind me.

I learned that my daughter, Kamryn, was asthmatic at five years old. She was now fourteen and had mostly grown out of it. But hot, pollen-filled days like today in Missouri triggered asthma and allergy symptoms for everyone.

Earlier that morning, I'd taken every precaution to

ensure she would have no issues during the soccer tournament. Unfortunately, the oral medication, albuterol treatment, and homeopathic methods hadn't worked today.

"Her backpack!" I screamed, still running onto the field. "The inhaler is in her backpack."

By then, I could hear the ambulance and see my child's limp body lying on the grass field. People were gathered around her, while her father yelled for them to back up.

Parting the crowd, I crumbled to the ground and immediately began praying. I knew that it was too late for the inhaler because my Kami wasn't even gasping for breath at that point.

"Please! Back up! Everybody back!" a deep voice commanded.

If I hadn't been in such a panic, I would've allowed my eyes to linger on the fine man before me dressed in blue pants, black Timberland boots, and a white tank. A silver shield hung from a chain around his neck, and thick locs swung freely around his face. But even through panic, I noticed him.

The stranger didn't say another word as he knelt over my daughter and began CPR. His oversized palms pressed into her small chest, over and over again. Only seconds passed, but an eternity flashed before my eyes. *What would I do without my Kami?*

Tears blurred my vision, so I thought I was dreaming when her chest jumped, then jumped again. She was coughing. She was breathing.

"Kam. Babygirl," I heard her father say as he pulled her into his arms.

"Sir. Sir," the bass-filled voice called. "Please let the EMTs take her to the hospital," he continued, gently removing my daughter from her father's grasp.

I noticed two other people lifting Kamryn onto the stretcher. They were dressed similarly to the stranger, except they wore blue uniform shirts.

"Lyn, go with Kam. I'll follow you," Sonny said.

It took me a moment to get my bearings, but I quickly jolted from my daze and climbed into the ambulance to join my daughter.

Hours later, Kamryn was awake and in good spirits. She had some chest pain from the compressions, but overall, she was fine. The emergency room doctor wanted to keep her overnight for observation, so I camped out in her room.

The medication pumping through the IV made her hyper, so Kami was Chatty Cathy for about an hour before finally falling asleep. I quickly followed her lead, curled uncomfortably in the chair.

I was awakened by gentle taps on my shoulder. Through narrowed eyes, I caught glimpses of the stranger. The white T-shirt that had clung to his broad physique was now hidden beneath a blue uniform shirt, and a bundle of locs was pulled back into a bun. His skin was smooth, his features youthful—appearing too young to cause the tingling between my legs. This time I saw the name *Raymond* on his shirt.

"Someone can get you a cot. It may be a bit more comfortable than this chair," he said, his voice gruff.

"What time is it?" I rasped, slowly waking from the haze.

"Midnight. They'll probably let her rest here until it's time for discharge."

I nodded.

"Thank you," I whispered.

"No problem. I'll get the cot and more blankets," he said, turning to walk away.

"No, wait," I said, clearing my throat. "Thank you. You saved my baby's life." My voice quivered.

He shrugged. "Just doing my job."

"Where did you come from?" I blurted, not wanting him to leave yet. "You were there before the ambulance."

"Across the field. I'd just gotten off duty and was about to play flag football with some friends when I heard the commotion."

"Wow," I breathed.

Rubbing a hand down my face, I exhaled, unable to silence the wail threatening to escape. My lips trembled, and I dropped my head into my palm to hide the emotion.

"Your daughter is going to be fine, Miss. I promise," he said with certainty.

The stranger didn't hesitate to pull me into a hug. Although his closeness should've felt inappropriate, the warmth of his body comforted me and calmed my worries.

I nodded, lifting my head from his chest. The moment our eyes met, something shifted. This stranger felt more like an intruder. One small nudge to my chin and he was stealing all of my common sense. He was a force. His pull was so magnetic, I instinctively moved closer. An *irresistible allure* controlling me.

What in the hell was going on? Why did I want to fuck this man—who looked more like a boy—in the empty hospital bed next door?

Hesitantly, I pulled away, because if he came one step closer, the life-saving stranger would be performing mouth-to-mouth on me for entirely different reasons.

"Thank you again, Raymond," I whispered.

His brow furrowed, then followed my gaze to the name printed on his shirt.

"My—" he started.

"How's our patient?" the nurse interrupted.

At the sound of her voice, Raymond and I jumped apart, putting distance between us. I nodded and smiled at the nurse.

"Getting some much-needed rest," I replied, walking to Kamryn's bedside.

I watched the nurse check her vitals and medication. Raymond stood beside me, then leaned over and whispered, "You're welcome. If you need... anything, give me a call."

He covertly slid a business card from his hand to mine. I glanced down to see the black card held only a phone number and an infinity symbol printed in gold. I turned to ask him about it, but he was gone.

## BLAIZE

"B. You have a new client," Tammy said as soon as I answered the phone.

"Hello to you too, Tam," I replied sarcastically. "New client," I repeated. "What's her name?"

"How do you know it's not a he?" she teased.

"Nah. To each his own, but you know I don't get down like that. They didn't call me 3P for nothing," I laughed.

Tammy laughed, too. "Pretty Pussy Penetrator," she said sarcastically. "That was so stupid. I'm glad you left that shit in high school."

Tamera Finch and I had been friends since eighth grade. Me, her, and Jordan were the Three Musketeers back then. While she and Jordan drifted apart after complicating things with sex in high school, Tammy and I remained close.

About six months ago, she presented me with a *proposal* to make some much-needed money. I worked for pennies as an EMT while paying my way through college. My financial situation was rough, and I was willing to do just about anything to pull myself out of the hole—aside from asking my parents for help.

Tam had always been secretive about her job, but she was clearly about her business—townhouse, nice car, and all the latest designer items. The crew jokingly called her Tommy from *Martin* because we were convinced she didn't have a real job.

But she *did* a job. A lucrative one. Tammy headed up operations for an escort service called *Infinite Experiences*.

The service catered to busy women and men looking for a customized and discreet experience. Whether it was an occasional good time in bed, a weekend getaway, or a dinner date during a business trip, Infinite handled everyone's needs.

"So again I ask, what's her name, Tam?"

"Ice," Tammy answered. "She asked for Raymond," she added, brow furrowed.

A wide grin spread across my face. I'd been waiting for this call. *Raymond.* I laughed at the thought of her calling me by my last name. When I tried to correct her, the nurse interrupted us. But for her... I'd be Raymond.

The one afternoon I'd had off in weeks ended with me responding to a young girl in the throes of a serious asthma attack. I immediately noticed the woman crying and praying over her, but I couldn't focus on how damn fine she was in the middle of a crisis. But I noticed.

Instead of going home to get some sleep, I stayed at the hospital until I received an update on the patient. She was stable, and I was thankful. Standing in the threshold of the hospital room, I scanned the beautiful woman—who had to be the patient's mother—from head to toe.

She was magnificent. Even curled awkwardly in the hospital chair with her mouth slightly open, she was stunning. I told myself to walk away, but I couldn't resist waking her. From the moment her sleepy, red eyes landed on me, the fire blazing between us was scorching, making me wonder what she tasted like... what she felt like.

I could've walked away. Hell, I should've. But there was *something* about the woman I now knew as Ice. I had no expectations when I gave her my card. If she called, great—we'd have a little fun. If she didn't, I was sure we'd meet again one day.

But she called. And I was ready to oblige her every desire.

Dialing the number Tammy gave me, I waited through a few rings before a raspy voice greeted me.

"Ms. Ice. This is Raymond," I said.

"It's Madame Ice to you."


## ICELYN

Room 1210 felt a mile away when I stepped off the elevator at the Hilton Hotel on the complete opposite side of town. I'd accomplished nothing at work all day in anticipation of meeting Ray. And here I was, creeping with I man I'd only laid eyes on one time.

When I dialed the number on the card he gave me at the hospital, I had no idea the infinity symbol represented an escort service. The young woman who answered my call described their services as "high-end luxury companion-ship." I had no clue what that meant, but instead of hanging up immediately, my dumb ass made a request for Raymond's *services*.

I figured it had to be a joke and never expected him to call. But curiosity was definitely peaked. Almost two weeks passed and I hadn't heard anything about my request. I tried my best to erase him from my mind, but thoughts of the mahogany-hued god who was built like a warrior played repeatedly like a soothing melody.

He was beautiful, sexy... and kind. I still couldn't believe he stayed at the hospital to make sure Kam was okay. Maybe that was the allure? I was fascinated by his kindness and goodwill. Who was I kidding? I was fascinated by the relentless thoughts of what that dick could do.

So imagine my surprise when a call from an *unknown number* lit up my screen a little before midnight on a random Tuesday.

"Hello," I answered groggily, even though I wasn't asleep.

"Is this Ice?" a deep baritone voice asked.

I shot up in bed at the familiar raspy bass. "Um, yeah. Yes, this is Ice," I stammered, unable to steady the nervous flutter in my chest.

"Well, hello. This is Ray," he said.

His voice wrapped around me like silk. Every syllable rolled off his tongue with a smooth richness that sent shivers straight to my center.

"I understand you made a special request for me, Ms. Ice," he continued.

I nodded before humming, "Mmhmm. I did." I cleared my throat.

I needed to get my shit together if I was really doing this. "And it's Madame Ice to you," I whispered, releasing the nervousness as I settled back into the pillows.

He chuckled. "Did I catch you at a bad time... Madame Ice?"

The way those two words rolled off his tongue sent a

quiver through me. I exhaled slowly, taking a moment to collect myself. "No," I muttered. "Not at all."

"Good. Good." He paused, forcing us to sit in a second of anxiety-riddled silence—at least for me. "How's your daughter doing?" he asked.

My cheeks reddened as an unexpected ease washed over me. I was certain he could hear the smile in my voice, my appreciation for his concern unmistakable.

"She's doing really well. Thank you for asking. And thank you again for everything. I owe you."

Ray chuckled again. "Well… now we're getting to the real purpose of this call. I know exactly how you can repay me," he teased.

I didn't answer right away because *what the fuck* was all I could honestly muster. What was I doing? Was I really about to solicit the services of an escort? *Am I this woman?*

Yep, I decided before finally saying, "I'm listening."

Ray and I made plans to meet Friday night of that week because my kids would be with their dad. He offered to make reservations for dinner, but I swiftly declined. This wasn't a date. I needed to be kissed and cuddled and fucked with no expectations. And tonight was the night.

As per the contract, the agency, *Infinite Experiences*, made all the arrangements to ensure discretion. All I had to do was arrive, and the key would be waiting for me at the front desk. They even asked for emergency contact information, a detail that should have given me pause. But as much as I needed an uncomplicated release and how my body craved a relative stranger, my curiosity was equally piqued by the mysterious process unfolding before me.

Naturally, everything that could go wrong that day did, and I found myself arriving nearly an hour later than planned. Taking a deep breath, I tapped on the door although I had a key. My eyes darting anxiously from left to right down the hallway as if I would run into anyone I knew twenty miles away from my neighborhood. Nervous didn't even begin to describe how I felt. As outgoing, outspoken, and adventurous as I was, this situation pushed the limits... even for me.

Ray opened the door, dressed casually in a tank top and sweatpants. His tall, commanding presence was impossible to ignore. But it wasn't his impressive physique that caught my attention first. It was the radiant smile lighting his face, drawing me in completely, as if he was happy to see me.

"Madame Ice, it's good to see you again." His phone lifted almost melodically. But quickly shifted to a rumbling low baritone when he said, "You're as beautiful as I remember."

I tried my best to quell the goofy smile I felt forming. "Thank you. It's good to be seen," I said, but I wanted to scream *take me now*.

"Please. Come in," Ray said, stepping aside to let me into the suite.

My teeth grazed my bottom lip anxiously as my eyes swept across the room. The space was elegantly decorated, exuding both luxury and intimacy. I smiled to myself thinking, I guess this is what I paid for.

Across the room, a bottle of champagne sat in a bucket filled with ice. Two silver trays with water and other fixings were positioned on the table near the sliding patio doors. I couldn't move for a minute, avoiding looking at him as much as I could. Still clutching my bag, after a few moments of self-talk, I finally turned around, ready to take him in.

*Jesus be a fence.*

My breath stalled deep in my chest. Standing tall and commanding, his ebony locs hung freely, swaying slightly with each movement like ropes in a gentle breeze. His flawless dark onyx skin was mesmerizing, but it was his brilliant brown eyes that truly captivated me.

They sparkled with an irresistible mix of sexiness and boyish charm. A combination both disarming and dangerously attractive. *How old is he?* I'd been wondering about his age since we made these arrangements. I knew he was legal, but I couldn't quite place just how young he might be.

"Can I help you get comfortable?" he asked, holding a glass of champagne.

I'd been so enthralled in studying him that I hadn't noticed he'd opened the champagne bottle. I swallowed hard to settle the lump in my throat before nodding.

"How old are you?" I blurted before I could stop myself.

His mouth curved into a slow, sly grin, licking his tongue across his plump lips.

"Old enough to know exactly what you need... and how to give it to you, Madame Ice."

Ray slowly closed the distance between us, his presence commanding yet gentle. He slid my bag off my shoulder, his fingers brushing my skin as he eased off my blazer, revealing the delicate lace of my black bodysuit. The warmth of his touch sent goosebumps rippling across my skin, his surprisingly soft hands igniting heat beneath the surface.

"Relax. Let's have a good time tonight," he said, placing the flute in my hand.

I nodded, sipping the sweet bubbly, but damn, I wanted to toss it back like a shot of tequila. He took my other hand and guided me to the bedroom. After unbuttoning my jeans, he pressed lightly at my shoulder, encouraging me to sit on the bed. One at a time, Ray removed my heels, then slid my jeans down my thick thighs.

His eyes lit as they took me in, lingering like he was memorizing every curve. He caught his bottom lip between his teeth, and I knew he liked what he saw. I wasn't a small woman. My breasts were full, my hips generous, and my thighs? Ample enough to put a hurtin' on him.

Ready or not, he was about to handle all two hundred plus pounds of me. Judging by the hunger in his eyes, I'd say he was up for the challenge. Shit, was I ready though?

The bulge in his sweatpants left nothing to the imagination. He seemed to harden by the second, but his slow, deliberate movements told me he planned to take his time.

"Can... can I use the restroom real quick?" The words tumbled out. I slid off the bed, already halfway to the door. "I just want to freshen up," I added, grabbing my bag to take with me.

"Of course," he said. "But leave the bodysuit on." He winked.

A few minutes later, I stepped out of the bathroom wrapped in a sheer robe that matched my bodysuit. Ray's smile widened as his gaze swept over me. He held out his hand, and when I took it, he pulled me in gently, guiding me toward the living area.

We ate dinner, and to my surprise, the conversation was enjoyable. Nothing personal was shared, but we had a lot in common. After the third glass of champagne, my cackling was a clear sign all inhibitions had gone out the window.

I hummed along to the soft music drifting through the room. Ray extended his hand, lifting me from my seat. His hands settled at my waist, swaying us gently to the rhythm.

"Are you ready for me, Madame Ice?"

I nodded, but he shook his head, taking a step back. His retreat didn't stop him from brushing a finger from my ear down along my cheek before cupping my chin.

"No, ma'am. I need verbal consent," he said softly. "I know you signed an agreement, but I need to hear that you want this."

I nodded again, then forced the words out.

"Yes. I'm ready for you." I paused, meeting his eyes. "Any rules I missed in the contract? Anything off-limits?" I teased, though I meant it.

He shook his head. "Nah, nothing's off-limits with me, baby. But there is one rule."

My brows lifted, oddly excited by the idea of rules for a change.

"The only way I stop is if you say the safe word," he continued.

"And what word is that?" I asked, lost in the pools of chocolate he called eyes.

"You tell me. It's your choice."

Ray stepped deeper into my space, his eyes penetrating, his touch intoxicating. I tried to steady the rapid rise and fall of my chest as I searched for a word. But this man was like hot lava simmering beneath the surface. The gentlest touch seared me to my core.

"What's your safe word, Madame Ice?" he murmured, brushing his lips across my forehead.

"Fire."

## *blaize & icelyn*



## ICELYN

"SiSi," I whisper-yelled as she grinned in Jordan's face.

"SiSi," I grunted again, but she still ignored me.

Deciding to get aggressive, I yanked her arm in an attempt to pull her away from him.

"We need a minute. She'll be with you momentarily," I said with a smile but wasn't shit funny at all.

Shoving her into the nearest house, we walked down the corridor into one of the sitting areas.

"What is going on? I was trying to use a condom or two tonight, too," Sienna bantered.

"Fire," I blurted.

"Fire? What fire? Where?" she asked, suddenly frantic.

"Blaize *is* Fire," I continued, practically panting as I shifted side to side like I had to pee.

"Oh shit. You scared me," she exhaled, a hand to her heart. "But girl, we can all see that nigga is fire," she sang, stretching out the last word.

"You're not listening," I griped through clenched teeth. "Blaize is *my* fire."

My eyes widened, brows piqued as I silently hoped our best-friend telepathy would kick in like it always did.

With a furrowed brow, Sienna muttered, "My fire, my fire..." Then she blurted, "Your fire." Recognition brightened her face. "Oh shit... Fire! Blaize is your *smack-it-up, flip-it, rub-it-down* fire from all those years ago?" she whispered.

I nodded anxiously, swallowing hard to push the boulder from my lungs. The grin on my friend's face was eerie and a little sneaky.

"Seduction," she began singing Usher, grinding with that damn body roll again.

I laughed, playfully smacking her arm. "This is no time for jokes. What am I going to do?"

Sienna cocked her head. "Um... use every one of those condoms and all that damn lube you packed," she said matter-of-factly.

I rolled my eyes. "SiSi," I squealed irritably.

"You already know what that dick do, so what's the problem?" she asked.

"That *is* the problem. You don't remember how long it took me to stop thinking about that boy's dick?"

"I do." Sienna nodded.

"And do you remember how I wanted to stalk him?"

"I do." She nodded again.

"So this…" I stressed, erratically circling my finger around the room, "is not okay."

"Young tender done growed up though," Sienna joked, nibbling the tip of her nail. "I thought he had locs and a smooth baby face in your colorful stories."

"Because he did back then. His ass has definitely grown up. *My Lawd*," I whispered, tossing back a bottle of water.

"Lyn," Sienna said, snapping me out of my musing. "This could be a win-win situation. You're not a single mom raising teenage kids, and he's not a twenty-something trying to figure out his life." She nodded and shrugged, as if trying to get me to agree before she continued.

"If he can afford my prices for this trip, he clearly has his shit together. And besides, he's older now, which means he's probably some years mo' betta." She smacked her lips, sticking out her tongue.

I pursed my lips, considering her logic. When I met Raymond—*my Fire*—he was a twenty-eight-year-old EMT trying to figure out what he wanted to be when he grew up. I, on the other hand, was thirty-six, the mother of two active kids and in graduate school. Time was a hot commodity, and when I had it to give, I wanted it to be worth my while. And *Fire* offered exactly what I needed.

That young man knew the intricacies of my body like a man who'd mapped it in the dark a thousand times. Every soft rise. Every sweet hollow. Every place that made me cry out without meaning to. With just one touch, he could strip away my angst and have me melting before the door even clicked shut to the suite we shared every other weekend for almost six months.

*Hmm... maybe he'd be willing to take a slow, filthy stroll down memory lane.* I could almost feel his touch tracing the places he once claimed, as if they'd never stopped being his.

## BLAIZE

"Yo, dawg. Come here, man," I said to Jordan, the distress in my tone unmistakable.

He practically rolled his eyes as I pulled him away from an intense conversation with a pretty brown woman with a ginormous ass. I jerked my head away from the crowd, demanding he follow me.

"Dawg, I was about to hit that," Jordan crooned. "Did you see that shit trailing behind her?"

"It's Madame Ice," I interrupted before he went off on a tangent.

"What?" Jordan barked. "Nigga, who? What are you talking about?"

"The baddie I went to the beach with... She's Madame Ice. *My* Madame Ice," I stressed.

My eyes widened as they locked with Jordan's, waiting for him to acknowledge what the hell I'd just said.

"Baddie in the tight white dress?" he said.

I almost rolled my eyes like my babygirl at this stupid dude. "Bro, they *all* have on white dresses."

He nodded, realizing the obvious. A moment of silence stretched between us, and I could almost see the calculations spinning in his head. Like he was lining up my words with every wild story I'd ever told him.

"Oh shit!" Jordan paused, amusement and disbelief crossing his face. "You mean to tell me you've fucked that many women you didn't recognize her when you first saw her?"

"Nah, nigga. It's been a lot of years. She looks different. Still sexy as hell, but different."

"What triggered the memory then?" he asked.

I was immediately transported back to the beach, when our tongues collided in a delectable dance. Her lips were just as plump and soft as I remembered. But when she sucked my damn tongue... shit... no woman had perfected that move since Madame Ice.

"The kiss," I muttered. "I'll never forget how that shit felt," I added, swiping two fingers across my lips. My eyes wandered unconsciously, searching for her.

"So what's the issue?" Jordan probed.

"The issue..." My words lingered. "You remember how that grown-ass woman completely turned me out?"

Our connection was more than scheduled physical intimacy. Don't get me wrong, I sampled and sexed every orifice that woman had to offer. But I cherished the quiet nights when I could simply watch her sleep, and the tender mornings when the bubble we created was ours alone.

Even under unorthodox circumstances, Ice and I developed a friendship. Jordan was one of the few people who knew my past profession and the only one who knew about my short-lived yet undeniable bond with Madame Ice.

"Yep. I also recall you contemplating finding that woman right before Alyssa dropped the bomb named Blyss on you. Your circumstances are different now, bro. You're a grown-ass man who has his shit together." He lightly shoved my shoulder. "And we're in paradise, so make the best of that shit with some pussy you already know is superb," Jordan added bluntly.

I creased my brow because, as usual, his approach was crass... but maybe he wasn't wrong.

# *icelyn*

"Lord help me," I murmured as the steamy shower water massaged every inch of my body.

Day two. Only day two, and I was already ready to pack my shit and hop on the next flight out. Having Ray—Fire—Blaize, or whatever the hell he's calling himself now, here, in the flesh, had me completely unhinged. I'd done everything in my power to avoid that man last night, finally dragging myself to my room like hiding could fix it.

But I knew better. I couldn't dodge him forever. I took a deep breath and prepared myself for whatever the day would bring. The group was having breakfast at the ladies' house before the day's activities were revealed. The only instructions? Dress comfortably, wear sneakers, and bring a bathing suit.

I slid on my hot pink strapless romper over a two-piece swimsuit, added silver flip-flops, and tossed my colorful

Nikes, sunglasses, and lip gloss into my oversized tote. The smell of fresh coffee lured me toward the kitchen before I was even fully ready.

Chatter and laughter floated through the space, already thick with energy. The massive marble island was doing double duty holding a full breakfast spread while seating some of the group. Silver trays of eggs, hash browns, grits, bacon, sausage, French toast, and a rainbow of juices and champagne filled the room with warmth and temptation.

But I couldn't eat. Not until I found him. I needed to know where he was so I could avoid that panty-wetting smile and that voice that still echoes in the back of my damn mind. Just as soon as I thought it, his bass-filled laugh rolled in from the patio. I didn't even need to see his face. I *knew* that laugh.

Through the open doors, I spotted his broad back. Swim trunks and a matching tank clung to every curve of muscle he'd clearly been working on. He'd always been beautifully made, but damn, he was even better than I remembered. Stronger, sharper, and dangerous. His chocolate skin glistened under the morning sun, and I blinked rapidly, trying to snap myself out of it.

He hadn't noticed me yet, so I moved quickly, grabbing a coffee and a mimosa and filling a plate like I had somewhere to be. I turned to make my escape, slipping down the hallway toward the lounge when a voice called out—

"Icelyn, you're not joining us?" one of the ladies asked.

I slowly turned and there was Clarissa. And standing

right beside her... was Blaize. He didn't say a word. Just pierced me with those soulful, dark eyes.

"I was going to eat by the pool. I need some good D—um, I mean vitamin D. Sun. I need some sun," I stammered.

*Vitamin D, huh? Oh, I wanted some, all right.*

"Vitamin D... that sounds like a good idea," Blaize said casually, as if he hadn't just come from outside.

Setting his plate on the counter, he grabbed an apple from the basket and poured himself a glass of juice like this was just another ordinary day. But absolutely nothing about this was ordinary.

I huffed, feigning annoyance, but waited for him anyway before heading toward the pool. I walked just ahead of him, pausing when we reached the deck. Noticing a few others had the same idea, only one high-top table facing the beach was open. I tilted my head toward it. He nodded, extending his arm for me to lead the way.

Although my nerves were shot, I had to admit it was a glorious morning. The sun hung low, and the waves rolled in with their own rhythm. I took a deep breath, letting the fresh air settle my unease.

We didn't speak. We didn't even look at each other. When I shifted slightly to glance at him, his eyes were closed as he drew in a slow breath. It felt like we were both filling our lungs with everything the day had to give. Washing away any heaviness we'd been unknowingly carrying.

I closed my eyes, too, allowing the sunlight to warm my skin, as the first sip of coffee grounded me. Then his smooth, easy voice cut through the quiet.

"So... Ms. Ice. How long are you planning to ignore me?" Blaize said, his baritone low and unbothered.

"I'm not ignoring you," I replied blankly.

It was a lie through and through, and we both knew it.

"No?" he chuckled, raising a brow. "Could've fooled me. You were playing musical chairs all night just to avoid eye contact."

"This is just..." I started, but the words slipped away. I didn't know what to call this.

"Insane. Improbable." He leaned closer, his voice dipping lower. "Sexy as fuck."

I bit back a smile, nibbling my bottom lip. He felt it, too. I nodded. "Yeah. What are the odds, after all this time? Like ten years, right?"

"Twelve," he corrected. "We haven't crossed paths in twelve years... and now here we are."

"Here we are," I echoed, taking another sip from my mug.

Blaize reached out, took the cup from me, and placed it on the table. He grabbed the arm of my chair and pulled it closer until I was positioned between his strong thighs. He rested his hand on top of mine. His touch was warm, tender, and familiar.

"Ice, let's be real," he said, his tone serious yet gentle. "A lot has changed over the years... but not *this*. Not *us*. That kiss last night—" His voice trailed off, eyes fluttering shut before locking onto mine again. "Clear indication the magic we had? It's still here."

Blaize opened his hand and clasped mine. "Feel that?" he asked, and I did.

I'd felt that shit all night. I tossed and turned, a restless tingle between my legs. A pillow pressed there was the only relief.

He looked down, his gaze dropping to where our forearms touched, both covered in goosebumps. He brushed his fingers across my skin, steady and soft. A chill settled low in my belly, making me shiver. I couldn't hide the reaction, couldn't pretend I wasn't affected. Because the truth was... I *still* felt him.

I blushed because he was right. *Magically delicious* was the only way to describe what we'd shared. Ray—no, Blaize—wasn't just a paid companion back then. He was the man who saved my daughter's life. My friend. My lover. The man who made me feel *seen* even in moments I didn't realize I was shrinking.

I used to count down the days until my kids went to their father's house, because that meant I got to see him. Sure, he'd ravished my body in ways I still couldn't explain nor comprehend—not then, not now—but it wasn't just sex.

We *talked*. About school, his dreams, where to invest his money, which classes he should take, what kind of man he wanted to be. He trusted me. And I... I cared for him. That's why it had to end because it had become too real.

"Why don't we just get to know each other again?" he said, lifting my hand to kiss the palm. "Have some fun while we're in paradise."

He leaned back, eyes twinkling. "I don't know about you, but I *need* this vacation. And besides..."—his gaze swept across our surroundings before lowering to mine—"...we already know the sex is *superb,*" he whispered with a devilish smirk.

I gasped, then burst into laughter. "Ray—I mean Blaize—stop it," I hissed, pushing his arm playfully.

He cackled, showing off those perfect pearly whites. God, I remembered that smile. It used to light up the darkest parts of my day. The parts I didn't even know needed brightening.

"You can call me Ray..." he said, holding my gaze. "Or Fire." He winked.

Shaking my head, I focused on the beach. "I can't believe you let me call you that all that time," I giggled, blushing with embarrassment but also taking a moment to ponder his suggestion.

"I got used to it. And it was ours, you know? Nobody else has ever called me that—not to this day." Blaize's beautiful eyes stayed fixed on me, tracking every subtle movement.

*What do you have to lose, Icelyn? What's the worst that could happen?* I questioned silently. *A lot, bitch.*

Years ago, I stepped out of my comfort zone to have this man for just a moment in time. And that moment changed me forever. He lifted my body to heights I'm still coming down from. But more than that, we genuinely enjoyed each other's company. In another place and time, under very different circumstances, he could've been my forever. But just like back then, he was my *right now.* So I was going to live for right now.

"Yeah, okay. That sounds like a plan," I said with a casual shrug. "Let's have a good time. And after that, we can go back to not knowing each other again."

Blaize pursed his lips, nodding slowly. He reached out his hand, and I shook it, sealing the deal. But he didn't immediately let go. Instead, he held on a second too long, gently caressing my fingers before lifting my hand to his lips and placing a soft kiss in my palm. Then he rested it against the curve of his face.

The soft bristles of his beard against my skin sent shockwaves through my pussy. And just like that, I was melting. I felt it—that magnetic pull, a spark. That tingle along my spine that warned: Blaize Raymond was about to dickmatize me all over again.

He leaned back in his chair, a smug grin of victory on his face as he took a bite from the apple. *Damn you, forbidden fruit.*

We sat in silence for a few minutes, letting the breeze, the waves, and the quiet crackle of old chemistry fill the space between us.

"So... how's your daughter? Kerry or Kam?" he asked, dragging me out of my thoughts.

"Kamryn," I corrected with a nod. "She's good. Almost thirty and getting married." I tried to keep my tone light, but the last two words dripped with resignation.

"Wow. Congratulations," he said, but his enthusiasm faded when he caught my expression. "Not a happy occasion?"

I gave a half-hearted smile. "Let's just say... I'm not a fan of her fiancé. But that's neither here nor there."

He nodded, sensing not to push. "What about your son? I can't remember his name."

"Bryson. He just graduated from college and he's moving for a new job."

"That's amazing. Great work, Mom," Blaize said, holding his hand up for a high five.

I chuckled and smacked his palm.

"And you?" I asked, narrowing my eyes, curiosity lacing my tone. "What's been going on with you?"

He snickered. "Whew... a lot." He smiled, twirling the toothpick between his fingers. "I finished school. And I'm a dad."

"Wow. That's great. Congratulations on everything." I paused, genuinely happy for him. School had always been his primary goal when we knew each other, but becoming a father? That was icing on the cake if his beaming smile was any indication.

"Must be a girl," I said.

Blaize's eyes darted to mine. "How'd you know?"

"My daughter is a daddy's girl, and she leaves that same look on her father's face when he talks about her," I said with a chuckle. "What's her name?"

"Blyss." He smiled wide. "She's ten going on, shit, thirty. And the love of my life."

I blushed, completely understanding his sentiment, but still mesmerized by this grown-ass man before me.

"Wow. It's really been twelve years," I muttered.

He nodded. "Twelve years, Madame Ice."

Blaize held my gaze, the weight and passion living behind his eyes pressing into my chest, pulling me back to places I'd tried to forget. His lips parted like he had more to say but before he could, a voice behind us shattered the moment—

"Good morning, good morning!" Sienna yelped as the rest of the group made their way to the pool area. "Welcome to day two! Today is *pick your grown and sexy adventure.* You'll be divided into groups. Whatever number you pick is the crew you'll roll with for the day." She smiled, her eyes landing on random faces in the crowd. "Tonight, after you return, we've got a fun beach party planned, so enjoy, lovers and friends!" she sang, sashaying around the space as everyone lined up to draw a number.

Blaize and I were the last to pick. He reached into the basket for the guys, while I fished a folded slip from the ladies' bowl. We unfolded them at the same time, locked eyes, and whispered in unison, "One."

Sienna slid beside me like a gossiping ghost and whispered, "The heavens must really want that man to fuck you again."

I dropped my head, trying *and failing* to stifle my laughter.

"That's *exactly* what the heavens want," Blaize called over his shoulder, grabbing my plate and casually walking away.

SiSi's eyes bulged in shock.

"I *keep* telling your ass you don't know how to whisper," I muttered, rolling my eyes as I hurried to catch up with Group One.

# *blaize*

Once Icelyn and I agreed to truly embrace this trip, everything shifted. We moved through the days like old friends who'd just rediscovered how to laugh together. We were playful, light, damn near giddy, and full of unspoken memories.

In the past, our moments were tucked away in hotel rooms, dimly lit corners, or late night text messages. Borrowed time wrapped in secrecy. But day three of this excursion was different. *She* was different. I saw Icelyn in full color... vibrant, magnetic, and unafraid. Watching her come alive in the open air felt like discovering a whole new chapter of a book I thought I'd already read.

We spent the day living life to the fullest; zip lining through the trees, jet skiing across the waves, and riding dune buggies through a Bahamian cultural tour. When our guide gave us the choice to return to the mansions or spend the rest of the evening at Radio Beach, Icelyn and I didn't hesitate. The beach it was. A few cabanas had been reserved for our group, and luckily, only two other couples decided to stay, giving us each a cabana to ourselves.

After a day packed with back-to-back adventures, we were both exhausted and hungry. The waiter appeared almost instantly, and we ordered nearly everything on the menu, including a bottle of 1942 tequila.

Icelyn looked so serene as she gazed out at the ocean, her pretty face shaded by oversized Gucci sunglasses, her braids neatly pulled into a bun. With her eyes closed, she inhaled deeply, letting the salty ocean air occupy her lungs. The scent of the sea mingled with the soothing sound of the waves, lulling us both into a peaceful, almost meditative state. She meditated on the beach, and I found myself meditating on her.

In a slow, deliberate motion, she peeled off her romper, revealing that breathtaking body in a two-piece bathing suit. The sun kissed her smooth brown skin in all the right places, highlighting every natural curve from her full, generous breasts to shapely hips.

Even the soft fold of her stomach and the glint of the tiny gem nestled in her navel made my pulse dip, then spike. She was sensual without even trying. Her effortless magnetism had always been an aphrodisiac… and she knew it. Not in a boastful way, but in the way a grown woman moved when she was confident in her skin and owning her beauty.

"Oh my God, I could stay here forever," she exclaimed,

stretching her arms above her head, her face glowing with contentment.

I tore my gaze away from her, finally managing a nod. "Definitely."

"It's beautiful," she added, her eyes sweeping over the scenery.

"You're beautiful," I replied without thinking, watching as a blush crept across her cheeks.

I patted the empty space beside me on the lounge bed, tilting my head in invitation. To my pleasant surprise, she didn't hesitate. Ice slid in next to me with an easy smile, the same one from years ago that always managed to undo me a little. My arm moved instinctively, curling around her shoulders as my hand traced gentle lines up and down her arm.

We sat in quiet companionship, taking in the view. The shimmering stretch of sand melting into the crystal-blue ocean. It was peaceful and still. Like time had hit pause just for us.

Our serenity was momentarily interrupted when the waitstaff appeared, balancing trays of sizzling food. Our overindulgence was apparent given the cloud of steam rising from the varying plates. We exchanged a look, laughter already dancing in our eyes.

"I think our eyes were bigger than our stomachs," she said, grinning.

"Speak for yourself. I'm about to kill this shit," I replied, pouring tequila into the shot glasses. I held mine up, and she followed suit. "To old friends and new memories," I said, my gaze holding on to the glimmer in her eyes.

Icelyn's smile softened, less flirtatious, but more of something I couldn't quite name.

"Cheers," she whispered.

We tossed them back in sync. In the stillness that followed, something unspoken settled between us. It was welcoming, intimate, and maybe a little too real. Icelyn broke the trance when she abruptly began removing the lids from our food. I nodded absently and followed suit, understanding that we... that *she* would need to take this slow.

An hour later, we were both pleasantly full and slightly tipsy after a few more shots of tequila and devouring some fire quesadillas, nachos, and steak tacos. The sky above us was a breathtaking canvas of fiery colors as the sun slowly set over the beach.

By now, Ice's inhibitions had fully melted. With her lids low and hands weaving through her braids, she swayed to the rhythm pulsing from the beach bar just feet away. I watched her, mesmerized, as the rest of the world blurred into silence.

Then she caught me looking, and that was all it took. With an unhurried, sexy grind, she made her way back toward me, hips moving in time with the music. Climbing onto the cabana bed, she curled against my bare chest like she belonged there. Her soft as silk skin molded perfectly to mine.

I pressed a kiss to her temple before murmuring, "Hey."

"Hmm," she hissed, tilting her head to look at me. The heat in her eyes matching the warmth in my chest.

"Come give me a kiss," I said, the words barely above a murmur.

There was already barely enough space between us for the night's breeze, so she didn't have far to go. A smile curved her pouty lips before she leaned in, happy to obey. The first few kisses were tender, slow, and intentional, but each one awakened all of my senses.

**Smell.** I inhaled deeply. The intoxicating scent of honey and wildflowers flooded my lungs, leaving me dizzy with desire.

**Touch.** The tips of her stiletto nails grazed my abdomen, sending shivers down my spine and pulling a guttural groan from my throat.

**Taste.** Our lips moved in a synchronized dance; tequila and temptation lingered on our tongues. The taste of her was pure bliss.

**Sound.** Her faint moans echoed like a sweet melody in my ears as I gently sucked her tongue.

**Sight.** The way arousal warmed her cheeks, misted her skin, and painted every inch of her gorgeous face—it was the perfect reintroduction to my Madame Ice.

She was straddling me and my dick could not behave under this kind of pressure. Fisting a handful of braids, I gently pressed her forehead to mine. My voice dropped, low and thick with want.

"Did you think about me?" I asked, my palm resting firmly on the curve of her hip while I maneuvered the other around the nape of her neck.

She didn't answer right away, just stared at me like I was

the only man in existence.

"I said..." I leaned in, letting my lips brush hers. "... did you think about me?"

Her eyes, heavy with longing, locked onto mine. She nodded, her voice husky when she said. "Yes."

"Then show me, Ice," I murmured, my fingers tightening slightly behind her neck, pulling her mouth closer. "Show me how much you missed a nigga."

She moved with languid confidence, her tongue tracing the edge of my lips before capturing my bottom one between hers. She bit my lip, and I bit her ass right back. The tequila had us both unphased and unfiltered.

She let out a devilish chuckle before slowly pulling my tongue into her mouth. *Shit*, Ice wasn't playing fair. She sucked like she was savoring a favorite memory. Like she was sucking my dick. Taking it in and out of her warm mouth at a lazy, unhurried pace while she swayed her center back and forth over my hardened length.

This was the calculated, grown-woman shit that undid me. I remembered this part of her well. Her mouth play was never rushed. It was layered in meaning and rich with experience. Passionate... controlled... and fucking intoxicating.

She'd taught me what intimacy really meant. That it wasn't bravado, but attention that pleased a woman.

Listening.

Learning the language of her body until I could write entire sonnets with my hands and mouth alone.

Ice had once told me that real connection started in the mind. That if I wanted her body, I had to reach her soul first, and that was the sexiest thing a man could do. And I had. I knew the delicate edges of her needs, the places she held back, and the ones she wanted explored.

I didn't need to guess. I'd studied her like scripture and I always bowed my head to bless the food before I ate. And even after all this time, I remembered exactly how to bring her to her peak before dick even entered her atmosphere. Mental. Emotional. Physical. That was our connection. In that order.

Ice continued her tongue-lashing, her fingers cradling the sides of my face as if recalling every angle. Her perfect lips devoured mine, the kiss hungry and unrelenting while her eyes held a careful patience, guarding words her mouth wouldn't dare say.

*Goddamn.* She hadn't lost a thing. Not the rhythm, and damn sure not the heat. My mind relived every detail, and my dick... its recollection was even better. She gasped as my arousal pressed between her thighs, grazing her softest place. My swim trunks were supposed to be waterproof, but I could feel her wetness seeping through.

Her slow glide turned into a prowling grind along my length—up, down, then swivel around and around. Up, down... then around and around again. Her movements were taunting and tantalizing, choreographed to take us exactly where we both wanted to go. Euphoria.

Breaking the kiss, she settled back on her heels. Our lips were swollen with desire, heavy breaths mingling between us. Her pretty eyes focused on me, blazing with a fire so fierce, as they trailed down my chest, across my stomach, landing on the massive tent in my shorts that refused to be ignored.

Without a word, she ran two fingers across her lips, then down the dip between her breasts, across her belly, and between her thighs. Still watching me, she slipped those fingers beneath the edge of her bikini, pushing the fabric aside. Her breathing turned ragged, her lip caught between her teeth as she dipped into herself once... then twice... then again.

"Damn," I growled, licking my lips, my body tightening with the memory of her sweetness. I knew that taste. Knew it like a man knew his mama.

Slowly withdrawing her fingers, she whispered, "See," offering proof of just how much she missed me.

"Give me some," I begged.

Ice traced her fingers across my bottom lip before slipping them into my mouth. She tasted like temptation, and I wanted every inch of her ass... bad. But I wasn't trying to get us arrested on this beach.

The sun had already dipped down to take its rest, wrapping the cabana in shadows. That was the good news; no one could see us. The bad news? We couldn't see who might be coming either.

These past few days, I'd played it safe, relearning her, enjoying the rhythm of our reunion. But the truth was, I was aching for her. Desperate to feel that familiar wet heat wrapped around me again.

Following her lead, I slid a finger down the seam of her swimsuit, easing the silky fabric aside. My two middle fingers found her center, slipping in slowly, while my thumb massaged her clit.

"Fuck," we groaned in unison, then laughed quietly, the tension easing just enough to make room for the desire building between us.

She was soaked; rocking against my hand as her thick thighs rode my digits. *My God.* If she kept rolling her hips like that, I was going to risk it all—jail time, scandal, whatever.

She was close. I could feel it. I'd seen it before. Those beautiful eyes getting lost in the back of her head, her breaths staggered, her grip tightening around my wrist to hold me in place. She was about to come, and I wasn't about to let her do it alone.

"Ray... Blaize," she moaned, her voice breathy and unguarded.

A quiet smile tugged at the corner of my mouth, amused by how she stumbled between the past and present with my name.

"Mmm-hmm," I murmured back, lost in the moment.

"Right there. Baby, right there," she pleaded, her body contracting.

I twisted my fingers, sliding them in and out of her core with leisurely, yet purposeful strokes. The waves whispered and roared crashing gently against the shore with a steady hum as she reached the pinnacle. When she broke, she collapsed against me, burying her face in my neck to muffle the howl of her release.

"Mmmm," she exhaled. Sound raspy, raw, and trembling against my chest.

"I've got you," I whispered, pinching her clit gently between two fingers, coaxing every final tremor from her body.

With one hand gripping the curve of her ass and the other still nestled between her thighs, I made up my mind: I was going to fuck her right here, right now. Arrest be damned.

She melted against me, boneless and breathless. But I wasn't finished. Not yet. She'd gone limp in my arms, but I knew just how to bring her ass back to life.

Tenderly, she kissed my Adam's apple, then traced a path of soft kisses from one nipple to the other. Her fingers toyed with the waistband of my swim trunks, her goal was clear. I couldn't push them down fast enough. Releasing my hand from between her legs, I lifted her beautiful body gently, aching to feel her warmth wrap around me.

But just as I was about to usher us there, her hand pressed softly against the center of my chest.

"You sure?" she asked, her voice quieter than usual, almost unsure.

I bit the inside of my cheek, holding back a laugh. Not out of mockery, but surprise. Every single part of me wanted to shout, *What the fuck you mean? Hell yeah, I'm sure.* But instead, I leaned in, brushing my lips up her jaw to the shell of her ear and whispered, "Yeah, baby. I'm absolutely sure. Are you—"

Before I could even finish my thought, Icelyn—*my mutherfuckin' Madame Ice*—took control, wrapping her fingers around my dick, guiding me straight into the depths of her essence. The slide of her slick folds against me was raw and reckless. But the way she felt on contact? Made me willing to risk it all.

The tip was barely in when her lips parted, brows drawing tight, and her movements stilled as she adjusted to the stretch. Maybe she'd forgotten how big I was. But her body remembered. Her pussy welcomed me slowly, trapping me one inch at a time.

*icelyn*

The van ride back from the beach was quiet… at least from our end. We collapsed into the backseat like two satisfied sinners, our bodies sun-kissed and worn from the day's adventure and the night's love making. Who was I fooling? That was straight fucking.

We'd barely come up for air before the world around us started to stir again. Just before the waiter cleared his throat and stepped around the cabana, I had just eased off of him, my body still humming from the high we'd just come down from.

The van rocked from the gravel road leading to our mansions. I must've drifted off at some point, because the next thing I remembered was the soft brush of his fingers on my thigh and the sound of the mansion's music floating through the open van doors.

Back at the house, the party was still in full swing. Folks

were posted up in the oversized lounge chairs, sipping drinks and swapping secrets. Others were in the pool, half-dressed, and playing games that had very little to do with winning and everything to do with teasing. It was giving summer camp for grown folks... complete with cat-and-mouse seduction.

I'd just grabbed a bottle of water from the cooler when Nicole strolled up, her lashes fluttering with curiosity and just enough mess.

"Girl, you ran off last night before the real fun started," she said, smirking. "Don't tell me you already got your eye on somebody."

Before I could even entertain her nosey-ass questions, Blaize appeared behind me like a shadow with heat.

"Madame Ice..." His deep voice skimmed across my skin like velvet. "Your presence is needed... Now."

Nicole's eyes bounced between us, her lips curving in a knowing smile. It was apparent that Blaize and I had found our own red, white, and blue fireworks for the night.

I didn't say a word. I didn't have to. I simply smiled at Nicole and followed Blaize through the house and up the stairs, both of us moving with the urgent, electric energy of two people who knew exactly what was about to happen... again.

As soon as we stepped into my room, he kicked the door shut and pressed me against it like he'd been holding back since the moment we met eyes again. Shit, since just an hour ago on the beach.

His hot and hungry lips crashed into mine. It was like our

time at the beach was child's play. This man was reckless and needy and damn near trembling with anticipation.

One hand cradled the back of my head while the other grabbed his favorite place... my ass, kneading it like he paid rent there. And my vagina was already dripping in it... again. *Perimenopausal dryness my ass.* I laughed internally at that because I knew that I would be searching for my bottle of lube very soon.

His dick lay thick and heavy against my stomach, and I swear I called for Jesus. Not in vain. Not in fear, but in reverence. A full acknowledgment of the divine assignment poised between my legs.

Something about this felt... different. Yes, I'd felt his impressive length earlier when I rode him in the cabana, but now? The way he was looking at me—locked in, hungry, almost devilish—I knew I was in for a wild night. And I should probably call for help. Immediately.

"Um... I— I'm going to need lubrication," I whispered breathlessly, barely able to finish the sentence.

"Let me take care of you, Ice. I'll get you whatever you need," he murmured, voice dipped in promise.

And with that, he dropped to his knees like a man on a mission. Like my body was his altar. He slid my bikini bottom down with a sluggishness that made heat creep up my spine, then pressed his lips reverently against my tender, sensitive center.

His tongue moved with intention, kissing every fold, every crevice, like he was reacquainting himself with a place he'd never stopped craving. My fingers gripped the door frame for balance as my knees threatened to give out, trembling from the building pleasure.

I was done. Shit... undone. Completely unraveled by a man who was worshiping my body like a prayer he could only whisper. Just as I teetered on the edge of a scream, Blaize rose like a wave and scooped my thick frame into his arms like it was nothing.

I'd lost a bit of weight since the last time he'd seen me, but I was no dainty lil' flower. I was still a whole lot of woman to have and to hold. A surprised laugh slipped out before I could stop it. Lord, I'd forgotten he had that kind of strength... and the nerve to use it on me.

"What's funny?" he asked, holding me mid-air like I was a featherweight.

I shook my head, breathless but smiling.

"Nothing," I giggled, the blush already creeping up my neck. "Just... remembering the good old days."

His lips curved into a knowing smirk.

"Oh yeah?" he said, kissing me slowly. "Let's make some new ones."

He carried me across the room, and my back met the glass patio door with a soft thud. The blinds were wide open, the glow from the pool below spilling into the room, and the sound of laughter drifting up from the partygoers outside.

Anyone could look up and see. And I hated to admit it, but the thought of someone catching even a glimpse of us like this made my clit throb harder. Before I could take a full breath, he was inside me, stealing the air from my lungs all over again.

Blaize was fucking me deep, firm, and unceasing. There was no hesitation. No teasing foreplay. Just a powerful rhythm that spoke of history, desire, and something neither of us had words for.

I locked my legs around his waist, not just to stay grounded, but to keep us connected to whatever this was. I didn't resist. I couldn't. I took all of him. Welcomed the swell, the fullness, the way my body molded to his like it had been waiting.

What happened on the beach *was* child's play. A tempting preview of everything still simmering between us. But what was happening now wasn't just lust for a long-lost lover. It was something *deeper*, something carved from memory and wrapped in meaning.

This wasn't about desire alone; it was recognition. Nostalgia. I squeezed my eyes shut, not just in response to the heaviness of him pounding my pussy, but to block out the memory of how it all ended with Blaize.

Right now, I didn't want to evoke the pain I masked. I wanted to feel *this*. Feel *him*. To savor the moment and surrender, fully and without wavering... even if it was only for the next couple of days.

"Goddamn," he groaned, his voice vibrating against the slope of my neck as he thrust in deeper, then slower... then in a pace my body could barely keep up with.

In and out. Up and down. Round and round. He was searching, fucking, digging for that spot he used to own.

"Ray..." I whimpered, my voice stretched thin and shaky through another release.

He chuckled low against my skin, lips trailing across my collarbone as his hips moved with determined purpose. I was going to get his name right one of these days, but right now, I could barely remember my own.

We stayed tangled together, our bodies molded together as his climax shuddered through his immense frame. Oh my God... I damn near cried when a gentle wave of creamy warmth slid down my pussy.

When his breathing finally steadied, he eased me back to my feet but didn't let go. Spinning me in his arms, he kept his hold firm around my waist, face buried in my hair then the misted curve of my neck before kissing down my shoulder.

With sluggish, delicate steps, he guided us toward the bathroom, our skin still humming from the heat we'd just shared. The cool tile against my bare feet sent a shiver racing across my skin. One glance at my reflection in the mirror had me snickering under my breath.

My braids were a wild, glorious mess. My bikini top was long gone, surrendered somewhere in the chaos, leaving my breasts full and uncontained. My skin was flushed, my bare ass on shameless display, and my thighs slick with the proof that Blaize still knew my body like no time had passed at all.

He lifted me onto the counter, and I watched in silence as he moved around the space with an easy confidence. God, this man was beautiful. Like somebody poured dark chocolate poured over steel.

His body was harder now, more chiseled than I remembered, and his skin mapped with new tattoos. The mix of affirmations and scripture inked across his torso had always drawn me in, each one telling a story I loved to trace with my fingertips.

Turning on the shower, he crossed the expanse of the bathroom and pulled fresh towels from the linen closet. When he stepped back between my legs, the air shifted. He kissed the tip of my nose before reaching around me for something. A second later, he held a makeup removal cloth in his hand. Blaize swept it across my skin with such deliberate gentleness that my belly quivered.

My lips curled into a slow smile as I tucked my bottom lip between my teeth. And then the memory hit me like a flash. Warm water cascading over our bodies, the room bathed in shadows, his quiet care lingering long after the rush had faded. That was always the thing about Blaize, he didn't just make love to my body. He *tended* to it.

Steam clouded the mirror, but I wasn't looking at my reflection anymore. My mind drifted twelve years back. To a suite in that downtown hotel with dim lighting and too-soft sheets. I'd had one of those soul-draining days where I questioned everything. The job. The routine. The way I was giving to everyone but myself.

The moment he opened the door, I collapsed into his arms, tears slipping down my cheeks as I confessed I wanted out. Out of the grind. Out of the life that left no room for my own dreams. I wanted to start my own business, build something that was mine but I couldn't. Not then. My babies were still in middle and high school, and braces, soccer and baseball fees, and college tours left no space for risk.

He held me like every word mattered. Like he saw something in me I hadn't dared to fully see yet. He didn't try to fix it or feed me some canned motivational speech. He just listened... and told me I was allowed to feel this.

*"You're capable of doing whatever you want to, Ice. You've got the vision, and you've got the heart. Your time's coming, baby. I promise."*

Nights like that made it easy to forget our arrangement was temporary. That whatever we had came with an expiration date. But when he spoke to me like that? When he looked at me like I was more? I let myself believe it and that terrified me.

Later, after he'd made love to me with the kind of tenderness I didn't know I needed nor deserved, he scooped me up and carried me to the bathroom. His arms were always steady... always sure. Followed by the same quiet whisper against my ear—

*"Let me take care of you, Madame Ice."*

And he did just that. Ray... *Blaize*... would run a bath, ease me into the water, and wash me with a kind of intimacy that felt like it needed to be earned. His hands glided over my skin like they were following a map he never wanted to forget. Lingering here, caressing there, each touch patient and willful.

*"You never rush," I murmured, my eyes fluttering closed as steam curled around us.*

*"You taught me to slow down," he said, his mouth quirking into that lazy smile before he winked.*

I smiled, tucking the moment away like a secret keepsake. Every other weekend with him had been my exhale.

With him, I could breathe. He wasn't just an escort. He was my safe place, my indulgence wrapped in enticement.

*"I see you, Ice,"* he whispered, brushing a kiss against my shoulder, his voice a low hum in my ear. *"You deserve this."*

*"I deserve what?" My lids were heavy, but curiosity cracked them open.*

*"Care," he said simply, as if that one word explained everything. And in that moment, it did.*

"Icelyn," his voice called me back to the now.

I blinked, the memory melting into steam as I turned my head. He stood just outside the shower, hand outstretched toward me. A smile tugged at my lips.

"Another smile. What is this one for?" he asked, his voice playful.

"Just thinking about aftercare," I said softly.

His cheeks lifted into a sexy grin. Those bright white teeth flashing against his rich, chocolate skin. Taking a slow step forward, his eyes darkened with mischief and promise.

"Aftercare is coming. I promise," he murmured. "But I'm not finished with you yet."

The tepid shower tile met my back as the water hissed, steam rising quickly, fogging the glass, and wrapping us in our own private haze. We stepped beneath the spray, letting it rinse away the sweat and salt of desire. But no matter how thoroughly we scrubbed or rinsed, the fever between us remained. An ache that water couldn't cool.

We kissed and lived in each other's arms as the water poured over us like a healing spring. With my cheek pressed to the wall, his firm but tender touch, shouldn't have felt so loving. But it did.

His lips wandered in a languid descent down my body, pausing just long enough to make me desperate for the next kiss. He was tasting me, shit, teasing me like he had all the time in the world. I couldn't do anything but release a weak moan.

"Blaize."

His hands claimed my ass like they were specially sculpted for it, fingers digging into my flesh as if he never intended to let go. Then his mouth was on me. So hot… so commanding as his tongue slid down my slit with deliberate focus. He tarried there, slowly exploring, savoring the moment until my body betrayed me with sharp, ragged gasps. This man was eating me from behind and I couldn't contain my cry.

"Blaize," I whimpered, louder this time.

Twenty-something-year-old Ray had been nasty… but forty-year-old Blaize? He was downright *indecent*. Like he'd spent the last twelve years perfecting the art of ruin. Because right now? His ass was demolishing me.

My palms pressed to the shower glass for balance, the heat from my skin leaving faint handprints in the steam. Each moan fogged the air around me, each shift of his tongue making those prints smear as my arms gave way.

My knees trembled, but his grip on my waist kept me anchored, even as my mind threatened to float away. Every stroke, every flick made me weaker… and he knew it. He wanted me ruined, and Lord help me, I was already halfway there.

Gradually, he rose to his full height, kissing the sting of every place he'd just burned with his tongue. My body was trembling so he burrowed close to me like I was something rare, something to be adored.

I swear my heart flatlined for a beat when he coasted into me from behind. The slow ascent of his pleasure was devastatingly good. It wasn't rough. It wasn't rushed. It was quiet. Deep.

His thick length filled me, stretching me in places that had been hibernating since the last time he owned my body. And when my climax came, it wasn't gentle, it tore through me like a hurricane, dismantling every wall I'd built, leaving only the wreckage of ecstasy in its wake.

"Fire," I screamed, the word ripping from my throat.

"Is that your surrender, Icey baby?" he groaned against my ear, instinctively pausing his pursuit as if the word flipped a switch inside him.

*Icey baby?* That was new… and I liked it. The sound of it curled around my spine, drawing my mind away for a split second until his low hum rumbled against my skin, dragging me back.

"You want me to stop?" he asked again, his baritone serious this time.

"No. No—hell no," I gasped, my nails digging into him. "Don't stop. Don't you fucking stop."

I was breathless, my body trembling in his hold, but my orgasm wouldn't relent. Waves crashing over me, stealing the air from my lungs until my vision blurred and the world turned hazy around the edges.

I reached behind me, my nails raked his thighs, desperate to anchor myself as his own release began to overtake him. His body locked against mine, a deep, guttural sound rumbling from his chest while his warm gooeyness spilled inside me, and still, my body kept pulsing, wringing every last drop of him until I was dazed and blind to everything but this man holding me.

Afterward, I stepped out of the shower on wobbly legs, but he followed close behind, pressing his length against my back with no shame in his renewed want. Damn, maybe SiSi was right about him still fucking like he was thirty.

His hands glided down my damp skin, resting briefly on my stomach before dipping down to my swollen clit. The moment his fingers found their tempo, my eyes rolled back on an exasperated exhale. Another round was coming. He'd made that painfully clear.

I couldn't even remember how many times I'd achieved the ultimate release. And goddamn, my center was tingling again. But my body was exhausted. It needed more than a timeout. I needed an intermission. A reprieve. Maybe even a mercy rule.

Every one of my nerve endings was over-sensitized. My legs trembled like they'd forgotten how to hold me up, while my core still fluttered with the aftershocks of the storm he'd just set off.

"Blaize. Sweetie, I'm not thirty anymore," I groaned, half-laughing, half-pleading. "I need a minute... or sixty."

He snickered, those lazy eyes scanning me for even a flicker of energy.

"Madame Ice," he rumbled, his bassy tenor curling into my ear like silk-draped sin. "I thought you wanted aftercare?"

"I do," I said, my laugh laced with a whine. "But the way your hand is moving… that's not exactly a lullaby."

He chuckled low before pressing soft kisses down my spine, like he was leaving breadcrumbs for later.

"Well, maybe aftercare ain't what it used to be."

## blaize

Icelyn was so damn lethargic it was almost as if her legs and arms had stopped working. With my hand resting at the small of her back, I guided her body, wrapped in nothing but milk-chocolate skin, through the haze. She moved like every ounce of her had been poured out, leaving nothing but the whisper of her release.

I laid a towel across the mattress and eased her down, face first, her cheek sinking into the fabric. She didn't resist. She didn't need to. I believed she still trusted me. Icelyn always had, from the very beginning, and that trust had never stopped feeling like its own form of intimacy. It was as powerful as any kiss or touch.

The room smelled of salt, sweat, and her sweetness, and I swore I'd never get used to the way she let me undo her, only to hand me the right to piece her back together again. Her glorious, naked body layed still, anticipating what was to come.

The familiar shea butter oil waited on the nightstand. I grabbed the bottle, warming it between my palms before kneeling at the edge of the bed. Starting at her ankles, I worked my way up in slow, unhurried strokes sinking into her skin. Her calves. Her thighs. Her hips. I took my time.

I wasn't trying to spark her arousal again; I just wanted to care for her. To worship her in the only way I knew once the fire died down. My hands traced the curve of her back, gliding over every inch until she melted deeper into the towel beneath her. She let out a low, unguarded moan.

"Turn over for me," I whispered.

She shifted, her breathing deep and heavy, but she didn't protest. I started again. This time along the front of her body. Shoulders. Arms. Belly. Breasts. I didn't linger anywhere; I just made sure she felt favored over everything. Valued.

When I reached her feet, I held each one in my hands like it was sacred. I rubbed small circles into her soles until her toes curled slightly, and I knew she was close to sleep.

"Sit up for a sec," I murmured.

She blinked up at me, not immediately noticing the bonnet in my hand. I tucked her braids beneath the silky leopard-print fabric. I laughed as she tried her damndest not to blush, but the apples of her cheeks were as red as ripe cherries.

Gently laying her back down, I climbed in behind her, wrapping my arms around her waist and pulling her close.

For a moment, we just breathed in sync, her body warm against mine.

"Damn... I like this new aftercare," she murmured with a lazy chuckle.

I brushed a kiss over her shoulder. "Not new," I corrected softly. "You just forgot how it feels."

She shook her head weakly, the sound of her denial heavy with exhaustion. "No... I never forgot. Not once."

Shit, neither did I. And with her cuddled against me, I knew some things never fade. Not the memory. Not the feeling. And definitely not her.

The room was dim, the curtains pulled tight, barely a sliver of morning light slipping through the fabric. I blinked awake just as the mattress shifted. Icelyn climbed back into bed, her movements easy and familiar like she'd done it a hundred times before.

She slid beneath the covers without a word, nestling into me as if her body had always belonged there. Her sun-kissed skin warmed my chest, our legs instinctively tangling beneath the sheets. The silence wasn't awkward. It was full. Comforting in the way only two people with nothing to prove and everything to feel can understand.

I'd been reluctant to take this trip. Never imagined I'd be here, wrapped around a woman I once tried to forget. But the truth was, I never really did. Madame Ice carved out a permanent corner in my memory. I'd tucked her away for safekeeping, only visiting when I needed to remember what *real* used to feel like. She was my one sacred thing I could revisit when the world felt too hollow.

"You're still a morning person, I see?" she mumbled, her voice soft against my shoulder.

I smiled and kissed her temple. "Yeah. Midnight shifts make it hard to sleep in. Even on vacation."

She groaned, and I laughed lightly. "Still not a fan of mornings, I see."

Ice gave a lazy shake of her head, then looked up at me with those half-lidded eyes and pouty lips that used to wreck me. Still did, apparently. I leaned in and kissed her once. Then again. Just a simple peck, enough to satisfy the quiet craving building in my chest.

"Um, Mister... morning breath... yuck," she teased, wrinkling her nose.

"Oh, damn." I laughed, covering my mouth. "My bad."

I rolled out of bed, shuffled to the bathroom, brushed, rinsed, and returned minutes later with a fresh mouth and a mission. I crawled back in and hovered over her, kissing her softly before she could protest.

"Better?" I murmured.

She licked her lips. "Much."

I layed on my side, propped on one elbow, my fingers tracing lazy circles along her shoulder. The comfort between us made it easy to speak.

"You remember that night in the back of your car?" I asked, my voice low.

She snorted, yanking the sheet halfway over her face. "You mean the night we fogged up every window and almost got arrested by mall security?"

A deep, husky laugh escaped before I could stop it.

"That's the one. You had on that little red dress with the slit up the thigh. I swear, Ice, I blacked out when you climbed on top of me."

"I had one too many French 75s," she grinned.

"And those tequila shots didn't help," I added, nudging her playfully.

She tilted her head, smirking. "True. But I also recall that was the night I learned grown men cry."

She winked, and I bit back a groan because she wasn't wrong. That night, after a perfect dinner an hour outside town, she got impatient and reached over the console, unbuttoned my pants, and land straight-up sucked the life out of me.

The next thing I remembered was that red dress hiked high, the matching thong disappearing in her fat ass as she straddled me. I wasn't prepared for the way she rode me into oblivion. That night... I caught feelings—and yeah, maybe I shed a tear.

"Ha ha. Real funny," I chuckled, shaking my head. "You nearly had me in a chokehold that night."

We both fell quiet, lost in the memory. Because that night wasn't just another every-other-week hookup. It was unplanned and spontaneous. The kind of night that happens when two people realize they missed each other on an ordinary Wednesday.

That was also the first time I made love to my Madame Ice. Yeah, we'd fucked in the car. Shit, we'd fucked a lot. Those weekend escapes were wild, electric, unforgettable. But that night in the hotel room? Something shifted for me.

She wasn't just the woman I craved. She became the peace I didn't know I needed. From that moment on, Ice wasn't just a good time. She was the place I found myself wanting to return to... even when I knew I couldn't stay.

We layed there, face to face, my hand cradling her cheek while her fingers absently played in my beard. Our eyes locked, and in that silence, everything we hadn't said over a decade ago began screaming without a sound.

*Why didn't we fight for it?*

*Why did you let me go?*

*Why didn't I stop you?*

The questions hovered between us, heavy in the air, but neither of us moved to speak. Maybe because we already knew the answers. Or maybe because saying them aloud would shatter whatever *this* was. This fragile, stolen moment that felt too good to question.

Ice gave a small nod, blinking back the forming glaze in her eyes like she'd heard the hushed conversation in my head. Then, without speaking, she let her lashes fall and burrowed into the crook of my arm.

Avoidance. A signal that she wasn't ready to go deeper. Not yet. And maybe... I wasn't either. So I held her, letting the silence settle between us like a haze clinging to the water, soft and weightless, but ever-present.

# *icelyn*

Blaize slipped out mid-morning, leaving nothing behind but my aching thighs, the scent of his cologne, and the ghost of our conversation still hovering in the air. I pretended to be asleep, too cowardly to open that door. Too full to risk spilling everything I'd kept bottled for years. He didn't press me. Just kissed my forehead and whispered, "I'll see you later."

I stayed there a while, letting the sheets cool beside me before finally rolling out of bed and into the shower. The hot water worked over my aching body, soothing muscles I hadn't used that thoroughly in a long time.

*Whew.* We'd both gotten older. Learned a few new tricks along the way. But that man had aged like expensive bourbon—stronger, smoother, and oh-so delicious. There's something about a little wisdom paired with a well-placed stroke that'd humble a woman real quick. And a bitch was at his mercy.

I lathered myself in lotion and scented oil before slipping into a blood-red strapless one-piece that made me feel bold and sexy. Then I tugged on frayed denim shorts that hit just below the curve of my behind and piled my braids into a high bun.

Day three had arrived, and I was determined to face it with fresh energy. Even if my legs were still whispering Blaize's name. He'd spent every night since that first one in my bed, and each night had been a new adventure. A game of how many ways he could twist and turn me like a slinky.

Just as I reached for the door, a knock made me jump. I opened it, thinking it was Blaize, but secretly hoping the Energizer Bunny would give me a little reprieve.

"Put y'all clothes on!" Sienna's voice rang out, full of mischief.

I opened the door wider, laughing. "You're ridiculous."

She stepped in, sniffing animatedly, her eyes sweeping the room with full-on investigator vibes.

"I thought Hercules was gonna keep you locked up all day. Is your kitty cat okay, friend? You need a care package? A sitz bath? A wheelchair?"

"Sienna!" I shouted, shoving her playfully.

"I'm just sayin'," she cackled. "I know that boy is a beast."

I shook my head, face scrunched in agreement and disbelief. "A beast indeed, honey. Like Black Thor summoning the storm, lightning flashing in his eyes, chile."

"Just ready to tear shit up, huh?" She added.

We dissolved into giggles as I gave her the play-by-play. Well, the rated-R version because we definitely had some rated-X moments that were meant to stay private. She hung onto every nasty detail like it was tea hotter than the steam rising from the pancakes downstairs.

By the time Sienna and I strolled into the main house, the kitchen was already buzzing—laughter bouncing off the walls, the smell of bacon and coffee making my belly rumble. Most of the group had gathered around the brunch spread, clinking mimosa glasses and clowning like we weren't all over forty and partying well past our bedtime.

I didn't need to search for him because I could *feel* him. Shit, I could *smell* him. My eyes found Blaize the moment I stepped into the room. He stood by the coffee machine, black mug in hand, arms flexed just enough to make me forget every ounce of common sense. And when our eyes met? My whole damn body smiled.

Sienna clocked it instantly as we approached where he and Nicole were standing.

"Well damn, Blaize. You glowing. What y'all do yesterday? Become one with the dolphins or something?" SiSi joked.

He chuckled into his mug. "I became one with *something*," he said lowly, peeking at me over the rim with flirtatious eyes.

Nicole narrowed her eyes, darting them between me and Blaize like a nosy lil' auntie.

"Mmhmm," she hummed inquisitively, like she'd just

solved a mystery. "Y'all seem to always be missing at the same time. You ain't slick." She pointed an accusatory finger at me.

I just grinned and reached for a biscuit. "A lady never tells," I sang.

"Well, good thing yo' ass ain't a lady," Sienna quipped, her expression clearly saying, *I know you, heffa.*

I tried to keep it cute, but my face must've told on me because they weren't letting up. Still, I didn't care. Not today. Not after the night I'd had. And definitely not with Blaize watching me like I was still his favorite secret.

His eyes never left me. Not when I laughed too hard at Sienna's jokes. Not when I reached for the fruit tray. Not even when I avoided his gaze on purpose, just to feel the heat of it crawl up my neck anyway. He had *that look*. Like he was remembering every inch of me. And damn it... I was remembering, too.

Thankfully, Sienna tapped her glass with a fork to gather everyone's attention.

"Alright, y'all," she grinned. "Today is *Choose Your Grown & Sexy Adventure Day.*"

A collective hum of approval rippled through the crowd as she continued.

"Each couple, single, or entanglement—*no judgment*—gets to pick an experience. Spa day, wine tasting, sailing, horseback riding, or just lay your ass out by the pool and mind your business."

The room erupted into cheers, mock arguments, and

clinking glasses. Sienna raised hers one more time. "Pick your vibe. Just make sure it ends with a good story."

Laughter filled the space again, but my eyes peeked over my coffee cup and landed on Blaize. Something told me... we were about to write one hell of a chapter.

Later, I wandered into the sunroom, drawn by the quiet warmth and the view of the water stretching into the distance. That's where Blaize found me. He was holding two flutes of mimosa like a man on a mission.

"A pineapple mimosa with a shot of Tito's for the lady," he crooned.

I nodded my approval as he handed me the glass, his eyes soft but glinting with mischief.

"You hangin' with me today?"

I raised an eyebrow, taking a sip of the perfectly mixed drink. "Depends. What's on the agenda?"

"Horses. A massage. And then a little surprise." He winked, taking a sip.

I tilted my head, intrigued, lips curving into a smirk. "That surprise better involve great food."

He laughed. "Great food. Smooth wine. Peaceful surroundings... and me."

I sighed theatrically, pretending to be unimpressed. "Fine. But only because you said wine."

His snicker rumbled low. "Yeah, okay."

With a swift pull, he lifted me from my seat, my body colliding with his in one effortless move. He guided his hands from my waist to my hips, then to my ass, gripping just enough to remind me who I was dealing with. I swallowed hard, my breath betraying me.

"Adventure awaits you, Madame Ice," he whispered, his lips grazing my cheek like a promise.

And just like that, the line between playful banter and something far more dangerous blurred... but it was too late because my pussy was already on fire.

*Get it together, Ice... before you ruin another expensive bathing suit.*

# *blaize*

Day three was shaping up to be impressive. The moment I saw horseback riding on the beach was an option, I knew exactly what Icelyn and I would be doing. We rode along the cliffs, the horses trotting slow and steady as the wind carried the scent of salt and something like peace.

The ocean stretched beside us, waves crashing in a rhythm that somehow matched the beat of my thoughts—most of them centered on the woman riding just a few feet away. The beautiful white horse with pink ribbon threaded through its mane was her chariot for the day. The mare's snowy coat glistened in the sunlight, pristine and regal, like she'd been dressed for a parade.

She kept veering sideways, brushing against my stallion's flank like she couldn't resist him. My boy was jet black, muscled, and proud, his hooves digging into the sand with quiet authority. He snorted, neck bowing each time the mare drifted close, and I swear he was showing off for her. Just like I was for Icelyn.

"Tell your horse to stop flirting with my horse," she teased, tugging at the strap beneath her chin.

I glanced over, catching the lift of her brow and that carefree grin. "He can't help it. Your horse is beautiful. Don't hate on my guy for shooting his shot."

Icelyn tried to hide the blush blooming on her cheeks, but it was no use. Her smile widened as her long braids fell across her face. I couldn't stop myself from watching her move in rhythm with the horse—thick thighs gripping the saddle, the crochet cover-up barely disguising the curve beneath. I shifted subtly, adjusting as best I could. The steady rock and sway were not helping.

"Well, tell him not to give up too easily. He may still have a chance." She smirked, urging her horse slightly ahead of mine.

"Oh, no worries, love. Ain't no giving up this time."

Icelyn's head turned, her stare locking onto mine. I held it without flinching, because I meant what I said—and she knew I wasn't playing. The way things ended between us left too much undefined, too many words unsaid. This wasn't the moment to carve them out. But that moment was coming.

I gave her a single nod, then urged my stallion ahead. She didn't fire back with some slick remark. Instead, she let the silence pass between us. But silence had its own sound at times, and this time it was deafening.

The trail curved along the edge of the ocean, where the sand shifted from firm to soft with each step of the horses. The tide reached for the shore in long, lazy stretches, the crash and retreat of the waves falling into rhythm with the steady beat of the horses' hooves. The farther we rode, the smaller the world felt. Just the two of us, and for a moment, I remembered how much I loved that feeling.

The wind whipped through her braids as she turned toward the water, her laughter catching in the breeze every time my stallion drifted closer, closing the gap between us.

"Okay, now he's just showing off," she said, reaching over to pat his mane.

The simple contact nearly made my heart seize. Something so small, so innocent, but damn, it felt good to witness the tender side of my usually in-control, perfectly put-together Madame Ice.

We rode for nearly an hour, sometimes talking, sometimes letting the silent hum of the ocean fall over us. But it wasn't empty silence. It was full of things unspoken, memories that refused to fade, and a pull neither of us had the courage to name just yet.

When we circled back to the stables, I dismounted first and held out a hand to help her down. She took it without hesitation, sliding from the saddle and landing softly against my chest.

"Smooth landing," I murmured, staring down the bridge of my nose at her.

She looked up but didn't move from my grasp. "Guess I've still got it."

I smiled. "You always did," I said, biting my bottom lip.

She pulled back, but I didn't let go. Her hand lingered in mine as we started down a narrow, winding trail. Palm leaves rustled above us, the shade cooler than the sunlit ride. The turquoise ocean peeked through the trees, glinting like it was waiting for us.

Icelyn slowed when we reached the cove, her breath catching as she noticed the tucked-away paradise. A canopy draped in soft white fabric billowed gently in the breeze. Beneath it, two massage tables stood ready. The waves lapped gracefully, and somewhere nearby, a waterfall whispered in the distance. It felt like our own private, peaceful oasis.

Her lips parted. "Blaize... this is beautiful."

I stepped behind her, sweeping her braids over one shoulder to reveal the curve of the other. My lips brushed the bare warm skin there. "So are you."

Her body softened against mine before she slipped free, fingertips grazing the crisp white linen as if she needed proof it was real. "I can't believe you planned all this."

"I told you we were going to have a good time." I winked. "Massage first... then a little surprise after."

Her head tilted, suspicion sparking in her eyes. "What kind of surprise?"

I smirked, leaning in close. "The kind you don't want to miss."

We slipped behind the partition to change, her pretty eyes still glimmering with wonder. As we undressed, I realized this wasn't just some vacation hook-up we'd walk away from and pretend never happened. This was *more...* This was a reconnection. One I never thought I'd get back until she looked at me like I was more than a memory. More than a contractual agreement.

Three days ago, Ice was hiding from me. Now, she stood butt-ass naked in front of me, completely unbothered. I let my gaze trail one last time over the soft contour of her frame before she reached for the white towel, wrapping it around herself like she wasn't fully aware of the effect she had on me.

My manhood reacted instantly, hard and ready, the ache almost making me forget we weren't alone. Our masseuses were only a few feet away. Icelyn glanced back over her shoulder, eyes soft but teasing, lips curved in a knowing smirk that said without words: *I know you want all this ass.* And God, she was right. *Effortless sexy* clung to her like a second skin. She didn't even have to try.

I shook my head, stepping around the divider to follow her to the table. What I thought were two separate beds pushed together turned out to be one oversized massage bed for two. Sienna, or maybe her planning team, had really set this up like she wanted me to fuck her friend on this table.

Icelyn climbed on first, lying face down as her towel loosened. Her head rested in the cushioned support, arms relaxed at her sides, and already I could see her chest rising and falling in an easy beat. Comfort had claimed her. I adjusted my towel and stretched out beside her.

The massage therapists greeted us quietly, moving with the same respect as the hush of the cove. The ocean played background vocals, waves kissing the shore in time with the strokes of practiced hands easing tension from our muscles. I peeked over once and found Icelyn's sleepy gaze fixed on me.

"You good?" I whispered, not wanting to break the serenity.

She nodded, lips lifting in a relaxed smile. "Too good. I might fall asleep."

I chuckled. "That's allowed."

Her eyes fluttered closed, surrendering. I followed her lead, soaking in the rare stillness. The way her fingers curled when the masseuse found a tender spot, or the way her face softened as each breath drew deeper. Watching her let go was the best kind of foreplay.

A soft tap on the shoulder broke my spell, and we were guided to turn over. We moved in sync, transitioning at the same time. Icelyn clutched the sheet to cover herself, then giggled when it slipped and exposed one breast. I snickered, forcing myself not to touch it.

Instead, I stared at the canopy above us, white linen shifting with the breeze, sunlight filtering through like liquid gold. Peace settled into my bones, the kind I wasn't sure I'd ever felt before. Not like this. Not with anyone else, maybe other than my babygirl, Blyss.

When the massage ended, the masseuse thanked us softly and slipped away, leaving us alone. Icelyn stayed wrapped in the sheet like a mummy, her braids spilling around her.

"I needed that," she said finally, voice raspy.

"Me too." I leaned over and kissed her temple.

Her eyes were heavy-lidded, but they still sparkled with something more. Something insidious.

"I'm... ready for something," she whispered, her eyes tracing every inch of me before focusing on where my body betrayed me. My man was hard as steel and straining, just for her.

My brow lifted. "Here? You sure?"

She nodded, and we both glanced around the secluded cove. No one in sight. Just the hush of the tide rolling in and the sky melting into shades of gold and rose. Our eyes held that post-massage haze, bodies loose, limbs heavy in the best way. Icelyn's skin glowed beneath the fading sun, luminous and soft, and she was breathtaking.

I didn't hesitate. If Ice wanted me right here, who was I to deny her? Cupping her chin, I kissed her slowly at first, never breaking eye contact as our mouths met. The kiss deepened naturally, lips parting, tongues finding each other with familiar ease.

Time wasn't exactly on our side, but I intended to make every second count. I lifted the lightweight sheet draped over us and shifted above her, settling between her thighs. Her legs parted instinctively, welcoming me without a word. That silent invitation hit deeper than anything she could've said. And then I kissed her again, this time with all the hunger we'd been pretending not to carry all day.

Icelyn loved to toy with the hairs in my beard while she studied my face, fingertips grazing my jaw. As if she was reconciling Ray the boy with Blaize the man. Her gaze never wavered even when I slowly settled into her wetness and the connection between us was undeniable.

A low moan escaped us but it was swallowed by the rumble of the waves, belonging only to us. My muscles were loose from the massage, my thoughts hazy, my body heavy in the most delicious way. My strokes were downright sluggish, moving with unhurried intention.

I pumped into her essence slowly and listlessly. Even in our languid pace, sensation bloomed and built without force. I moaned, and she answered. She hissed softly, and I followed.

Our satisfaction rocked in quiet harmony. The ocean hummed behind us, our private orchestra. This wasn't loud intimacy. It wasn't frantic or famished. It was the kind that lives in stillness. In shared breath. In the way our fingers instinctively intertwined. In the synchronized swell and release of our chests.

Even the cadence of our climax aligned, and peace settled over us like a well-worn blanket. The moment was calm. No conversation needed. Just touch. Just closeness. Just the quiet, knowing that we were there together, under an open sky, held by the same hands, breathing the same air.

We lazed beneath the cabana far longer than we intended. Eventually, reality nudged us forward. It was time for the next adventure. I pressed a trail of lazy kisses along her shoulder, coaxing her back to life.

"You ready for your surprise?" I murmured.

"No," she groaned, the word dissolving into a sleepy whine. "I just want to sleep."

I laughed, brushing my lips over her shoulder again before nipping lightly. "Sleep when you die. Come on, love."

She huffed but pushed herself upright, limbs loose and deliciously heavy. We dressed in easy silence. Every time her braids slipped into her face, she side-eyed me when she caught me staring, that knowing smirk tugging at her mouth.

I slid in behind her under the guise of helping adjust her swimsuit, letting my hands linger a beat too long. She swatted at me, but the blush creeping up her cheeks betrayed her.

"At least give me a hint," she said, twisting her braids into a messy bun.

I tapped my chin thoughtfully. "Hmm... Summer."

She squinted. "That's not a hint."

"It's the only one you're getting."

Her expression shifted between curious, cautious, and intrigued.

I held out my hand. "Trust me." She hesitated just long enough to make it interesting... then slipped her fingers into mine.

We followed a narrow stone path carved between wild palms and cascading bougainvillea. Icelyn stayed close, our hands linked as we walked. I caught myself glancing at her more than once, smiling at the anticipation dancing across her face.

The air mingled with something sweet as we neared the bend. And then we turned the corner to reveal the surprise.

A private picnic waited on the cliff's edge overlooking the

ocean. A low table draped in sheer linen, scattered rose petals, and two glasses of rosé already sweating in the shade awaited us. A small speaker hummed soft rhythm and blues. The same playlist we used to fall asleep to during our hotel weekends. She froze then covered her mouth.

"Wait... is that—"

"Our *Summer in the Suite* playlist?" I finished, smiling. "Yeah. I found the files buried in an old email account."

Her hand stayed at her lips, eyes glistening as if the music had pulled her straight back in time. She looked at me, surprise flickering first... then something deeper.

"Blaize..."

"You told me that summer was the first time you'd ever felt calm," I said, walking her forward and pulling out a cushion for her. "Rested. I just wanted to give a little of that back to you."

But she didn't sit. She stood there, arms loosely wrapped around herself, taking it in — the table, the ocean stretching endless and turquoise below us, the wind, the music... and finally, me.

The breeze brushed her cheek at the same time my fingertip did. She let out a shaky laugh that trembled dangerously close to a sob. For a split second, I thought she might run. Bolt from whatever this moment was prying open inside her. But the emotion rising in her wasn't weakness. It was a reminder that beneath her armor still lived the woman who wanted to be *seen* and *touched* and *remembered*... and *chosen.*

I wanted to pull her in. Hold on and give her whatever

she needed. But I made myself stay still and let her decide if she would step closer. Her eyes softened. The wall between us cracked just enough for me to glimpse the woman I once knew. The one who believed in magic summers and quiet mornings of lovemaking wrapped in jazzy R&B.

"Don't cry, Ice," I teased gently, though my thumb itched to catch the tear threatening to spill.

"I'm not crying," she insisted, blinking too fast to make it believable.

"Alright," I murmured, letting her keep the lie.

I motioned for her to sit. She lowered herself slowly, and I followed. Our glasses waited, condensation sliding lazily down the stems. We lifted them, toasting to nothing in particular. Maybe to this breathtaking place. Maybe to surviving everything in between. Or maybe... to the possibility of second chances.

Her hand slipped onto my thigh, and she leaned into me. There was no urgency. No pressure. Just us. The rosé lingered on my tongue as the ocean scored our silence, waves rolling in steady devotion. And the playlist—*our playlist*—still knew every beat of us.

That's when it hit me. I wasn't trying to recreate a memory. I was building a new one. One we wouldn't have to leave behind this time.

# *blaize & icelyn*

## THE 4TH OF JULY

**ICELYN**

Every morning in Bimini had been peacefully quiet, but this morning was different. The ocean waves rocked in almost a ruckus rhythm as a light wind wailed. The sun splayed rays of orange and yellow, contrasting against a pearl-blue sky. Today, I watched the morning bloom from my bedroom balcony.

My eyes slowly lifted a little before six and landed on the beautiful figure sleeping next to me. Lying on his back, I traced the perfect lines of his chest and the ripples across his stomach. His tranquil nature should have calmed me. I wished the soft hum of Blaize's snore would've lulled me back to sleep. But instead, my mind spiraled, refusing to settle.

Today was the last day of *Seduction in Red, White, and*

*Blue*. The last day with Blaize. Just days ago, I wanted to hop on the first thing smoking to get out of here to avoid this man. And now I was desperate to press pause on the moment.

Blaize and I had a history that this weekend rekindled like a four-alarm fire. Even after all these years, we were still passionately dangerous for one another. But we... *I*, could not take this further. Tonight would be the end... again.

At least, that's what I kept telling myself as the waves rolled in, soft and unbothered, like they hadn't witnessed me lose all my good sense over this man. But I had to be realistic. These past few days—this vacation—were exactly that... an escape from the real world for a minute. A weekend of seduction with no questions asked. Not an opportunity for second chances or love connections.

I pulled my knees into my body, cradling myself as I rocked back and forth in the wicker chair. Inhaling deeply, I appreciated the purr of the wind. It barely brushed my cheek, but I felt its serenity. Then suddenly, a different sensation radiated. My skin prickled as a heat wave passed through me. Was it the sun? Was I having a hot flash?

And then, as if a voice whispered *Madame Ice*, I shifted to peer over my shoulder and met dark brown, curious eyes watching me. He didn't say a word or make a gesture, and neither did I. Our gazes collided for a long heartbeat; so many unspoken thoughts drifted in the air. With his head resting in the palm of one hand, he lifted the other, motioning for me to come to him.

I wished my feet were made of steel so I could stay

planted in that chair… keep my distance. But I forgot this man was magnetic. Magnets didn't chase. They don't stretch out a hand and demand surrender. They simply existed, forcing everything around them to respond.

And steel? Steel didn't stand a chance. The pull between a magnet and metal was strong enough to defy gravity. Strong enough to override logic. Strong enough to make resistance feel foolish.

So what did I do? I moved. Not rushed or frantic. I glided to him.

## BLAIZE

"What's on your mind, gorgeous?"

Icelyn was tucked beneath my arm, my lips resting against her temple. I'd woken to her side of the bed cool, clear evidence she'd been up for a while. For a split second, I forgot where I was. Then I *smelled* her. The breeze drifting in from the balcony carried lavender, shea butter, and something else I could only describe as comfort. It wrapped around me and pulled me fully awake.

I felt her head shift side to side, choosing silence instead of words. She was curled into me, her smooth back against my chest, bare ass pressed against my morning wood, her body molded to mine like it had found its rightful place. One leg draped lazily over mine, as if we'd been sleeping this way for years.

I chuckled softly, remembering how many mornings used to begin just like this. Back then, she'd sleep in while I woke early, content just watching her breathe, memorizing the stillness before the world came crashing in.

But today, my Madame Ice was the early riser. And if I knew her the way I thought I did, she was up because she was in her head. Hell... so was I. I kissed her shoulder lightly... a silent signal. She didn't have to explain. We didn't have to unpack anything right now. My heart was already doing too much.

Tonight was our last official night in Bimini. Tomorrow, everyone would scatter back to real life. Back to routines and responsibilities. But what about us? I wasn't saying we had to script forever. I just knew I didn't want this to be the last time I held her like this.

For years, we'd lived in the same city and never crossed paths. So finding her here? That didn't feel random. It felt... *intentional.* A blessing, even. At the very least, maybe we could be friends.

She shifted again, and I realized her breathing had deepened. She wasn't overthinking anymore. She was asleep. I eased out from behind her, careful not to disturb the warmth we'd created. Pulling on my shorts, I bent low and brushed a kiss across her forehead. My fingers lingered in her hair for a second longer than necessary. Then I kissed her once more and slipped out quietly.

## ICELYN

Sienna and her team curated an old-school barbecue straight out of a '90s family reunion, and it was exactly the distraction I needed. Blaize wanted to talk. Eventually, I knew I'd have to let him. But right now, this holiday kickback was the perfect remedy for both of us.

Grills sizzled with the best cuts of meat. A chef plated sides that tasted like somebody's grandmother had supervised the seasoning. The music shook the air, every version of the Electric Slide pulling people to the dance floor. Everyone showed up in their finest red, white, and blue, celebrating like freedom itself was on the menu.

I kept my distance, and Blaize let me. But not too much distance. We danced. He made me laugh. His hand would drift over my thigh or skim along my arm in that slow, deliberate way of his. So sultry and possessive like he was quietly reminding me where I used to belong. And I let him. Touch me like I was *still* his. Touch me like it might be the last time.

By sundown, we were drunk, loud, and ridiculous—accomplished professionals turned spring breakers raising our glasses to freedom, passion, and grown-folks business. That's when I felt him behind me. His deep, dangerous, bass-filled voice slid across the back of my neck like a slow exhale.

"Take a walk with me."

I turned. And there he was. The beautiful mess I once knew had grown into a beautiful man. I didn't hesitate. I slipped my hand into his, accepting the invitation without a word.

The beach glowed with bonfires and colored lights. Laughter spilled into the night as fireworks teased the horizon. We drifted far enough to hear ourselves over the noise. I pressed my back against his chest. His arms wrapped around my waist, his face settling into the curve of my neck. For a heartbeat, everything else faded. It was just us under the moonlight, hoping the sky might hand us what we couldn't say.

"Thank you," we whispered at the same time.

We laughed, allowing the tension to ease a bit. He turned me to face him, eyes searching mine. His tall frame bent slightly, his forehead resting gently against mine.

"I've thought about this, Ice," he murmured. "Not necessarily this exact moment, but... you. Us. Being with you again."

My breath left me shaky. My heart thudded so hard against my ribs I barely managed to choke out, "Ray—"

"Shh." He pressed a finger to my lips, shaking his head softly. "No need for a response right now. Just... let it be."

## BLAIZE

The bonfires and lanterns scattered along the sand suddenly felt small compared to the spectacle unraveling above us. Each explosion cracked the sky open, then spilled into showers of glitter that seemed to tumble straight into the water.

Gasps and cheers rose from the crowd down the beach, but between us, there was only quiet. My breath syncing with hers and the steady heat of her body pressed into mine. The finale boomed in a furious wash of red, white, and blue, so bright the water looked set aflame.

Sparks reflected on her skin, painting her in fleeting

bursts of color. Icelyn was devastatingly beautiful, her laughter hushed against the roar of the fireworks. I stared. I couldn't look away. I memorized her in that moment, locking it away like something I'd never let time erase.

One by one, onlookers began drifting back toward the villas. When she finally turned, I thought we'd linger, chat with the others, maybe slip into whatever after-hours party was waiting between the mansions. But she didn't stop. She didn't even glance around. She just caught my hand, gave the smallest tug, and led me wordlessly through the sand. Straight to my room.

We didn't speak. We didn't need to. The silence said everything—regret, gratitude, desire, fear. And under it all, something that scared the hell out of me: the possibility of love.

I kissed her like I had all the time in the world. Like memorizing her was my only job. Every stroke of my tongue against hers was patient and intentional. I wanted to own every second, because I knew that the moment would end.

The sex wasn't wild this time. It was a slow storm building. The air between us grew heavy and thick, yet a quiet breeze stirred, indicating something inevitable was coming. Every touch sparked like lightning flashing, stealing control from our limbs. Every kiss trembled, our mouths rumbled, growing more erratic, more restless like thunder closing in.

My mouth traced her like a map I'd lost but never forgotten, reclaiming ground that had always been mine. My hands moved over her with hunger, adoration, and need.

"You ruined me once. And you're doing it again," she

cried, her thighs trembling under the pressure of my tongue between her legs.

I looked up, locking on her gaze. My voice was low and assured. "Then let me finish what I started."

And I did.

I coaxed her open, my tongue and fingers moving to the beat that only the two of us could hear. I was patient but merciless until her body surrendered to me again and again. Every shiver, every gasp, was mine to claim. With each kiss, each stroke of my tongue, I told her the truth I'd been holding: *she was mine*. This was *ours*. Still alive. Still burning.

She might pretend tomorrow that she never heard the words I breathed against her skin, but tonight, I was done holding back. Tonight, I spoke with my hands, my mouth, my body, saying everything my heart had always wanted her to know.

Her body arched, her cries breaking like waves against me. She whispered my name, half prayer, half curse, clinging to me like I was salvation and sin rolled into one. I carried her through it, followed her into it, burying myself deep inside her until she couldn't tell where she ended and I began.

When release finally took us both, it was fierce and unrelenting. Our cries of pleasure and pain were swallowed by the thunder of fireworks exploding outside. But inside these walls, the blaze was ours. For one final night, we burned.

# SEVENTEEN

The sun came up too damn fast. Blaize was practically comatose after the night we had. I kissed his forehead, then his shoulder before slipping out of his room. My suitcase was still empty, and I needed time to pack before the car arrived. Quietly, I cracked the door, turning for one last look. My eyes grazed down the length of his milk-chocolate skin. With a smirk—equal parts fulfilled and afraid—I shut the door behind me.

In my room, I packed in silence. The calm of the past four days was already unraveling. Every folded shirt felt like I was leaving a piece of myself behind. By the time the knock came, I knew it was him. Of course it was him. He wouldn't just let me go.

"Come in," I called.

He leaned inside, hands stuffed in his pockets like a boy who didn't want to admit how much he cared.

"Hey," he said.

I smiled despite myself because he looked *good*. Black joggers and a plain white T-shirt fit his frame flawlessly. For some reason, the fitted cap turned backward and the glistening diamond earrings caused a stir in my center.

"Hey," I finally said.

"You good?" he asked, closing the door and leaning against it.

I nodded. "Almost done. The car will be here in twenty minutes."

"Cuttin' it close, huh?" He laughed, and I joined him.

"Always," I chuckled nervously.

Blaize flashed that slow, sensual smile at me, and something clenched low in my belly and deeper in my heart. But I didn't move. I forced my feet to stay rooted to the floor. I wanted to run. I wanted to scream. I wanted to fall apart in his arms. I wanted to rewind the clock and live these last four days again and again until time itself gave up on us.

"Come here, Ice."

When he opened his arms, resistance felt pointless. My body floated into his like it had been waiting all this time for the invitation. His lips brushed my hair, then lingered at my temple before finally finding my mouth.

"You weren't just a good time," he murmured against my skin. "Not now. Not back then. You were my peace. You were..." His voice trailed off when he caught the disbelief written across my face.

I pressed my head into the center of his chest. The space

between us was small, but the weight in the air felt suffocating.

"So why'd we let it go?" My question came out muffled but heavy.

An audible sigh slipped from his lips. "Because I wasn't ready for a woman like you," he said, his voice stripped bare. "You had your kids, your world. You were steady. And me? I was..."

After a few hushed seconds, I lifted my head and found his eyes fixed on some faraway place. I tilted his chin, forcing his gaze back to mine. "You were what?" I breathed.

"...Lost," he admitted, barely above a whisper. "I needed to find me."

Something in me trembled as his eyes searched mine, brimming with hope and want. Then he kissed me once more. The kiss was tender, filled with so much certainty.

"But now, I—"

"No." My voice cracked as I cut him off, tears stinging my eyes before they could spill.

"Ice. Baby—" His tone was rough, almost a growl, pleading with me to give him the answer he wanted before he'd even asked.

I shook my head, swallowing hard as my chest tightened. "No." The word broke again, softer this time but definitive.

I blinked, and the floodgate opened. Sniffing, I aggressively—angrily—swiped the tears away.

"Now *I'm* the lost one, Blaize." My shoulders lifted in a helpless shrug, a hollow laugh escaping even as my lips trembled. "And I need to find... me."

He thumbed my lips, trying to catch the salty tears, but it was no use. Pursing his own, he nodded, choosing not to battle me on this. Probably because he understood. I kissed his fingertips as they continued to skim my mouth and cheeks before I pulled back.

The silence between us screeched like nails on a chalkboard. I tossed the last few things into my bag while Blaize regarded me carefully. He stayed across the room, planted against the door, but I could feel his gaze marking my every move.

Zipping my suitcase, my hands paused when I felt him draw nearer. I closed my eyes, praying he'd shake some sense into me and let me go at the same time. Before I could lift it from the bed, his arm brushed the curve of my hip as he grabbed my luggage and wheeled it to the door.

"I'll be outside," he announced, then left me standing there—alone in my fault and feelings.

"Fuck," I whimpered.

Running a hand down my damp face, I snatched several tissues from the box and stuffed them into my tote before heading out. I knew this wouldn't be the last time I cried.

With oversized sunglasses covering half my face, I said my goodbyes, but the dark tint didn't hide a thing. My throat ached with unshed sobs as I smiled and nodded while people departed. Blaize stood by the car that would transport my group to the airport. Muscular arms crossed over his torso, he waited and watched me.

As I approached, I caught the flex of his jaw, tight enough I swore he'd crack a tooth. He lifted my sunglasses to peer into my reddened eyes. His closed-mouth smile was mostly sweet, mixed with a hint of disquiet. Sweeping his lips across the shell of my ear, he leaned in, not giving a damn who would see.

"Ice… are you sure?" he asked, the bass in his voice smooth as the crackle of a fireplace.

*Was I sure? Shit, I didn't know.* My heart screamed one thing, but my reality whispered another. My life was complicated, messy in ways I couldn't drag him into. Having Blaize in my orbit again would be more than a distraction… it would be an obsession. Shit, an all-consuming force.

We burned like flames clawing skyward, all heat and havoc, mind-blowing and destructive in the same breath. And as much as I craved it, as much as my body gravitated toward him like I was starving… I knew that wasn't what I needed. Not now.

I nodded, though my heart screamed no. "I'm sure. This was what it needed to be. A moment. A memory. That's all."

He answered with a single, measured dip of his chin. Cars rolled into the circular drive behind us, but we didn't care. He didn't. My tongue met his in the slow, familiar rhythm we'd perfected years ago. Care, sorrow, need all threaded through one last kiss.

Neither of us wanted to be the first to pull away but we finally did. I folded into his chest, pressing my cheek against him like I could anchor myself there. He dipped his head, brushing his nose along the crown of mine in that quiet, possessive way that always made my knees weak.

His thumb skimmed beneath my eye, catching a tear I hadn't realized had slipped free.

"Now see..." he murmured softly, tilting my chin up, "you gone mess up my dramatic exit."

I huffed a watery laugh just before he kissed me one last time.

"Take care of yourself, Madame Ice," he said, tapping the tip of my nose.

I smiled through the ache and brushed a kiss to his chin.

"You too, Blaize Raymond."

And just like that, we moved in opposite directions: me toward the car, him toward the house. I told myself not to look back. I didn't want to. But I couldn't close the door. Couldn't let the moment seal that easily. I thought he wouldn't turn around. But he did.

Our eyes caught one last time across the stretch of driveway. I lifted the corners of my mouth in something that tried to pass for resolve before finally shutting the door. Blaize stood on the step as the truck rolled forward, hands at his sides, watching. I watched, too, until distance swallowed him whole.

## *icelyn*



"Hey, stranger."

A raspy voice rang as I looked up from my phone to see Sienna. She strutted toward me, a scowl carved across her face. I stood, stuck out my bottom lip, and opened my arms for a hug.

"I'm sorry, bestie. My schedule's been insane," I sang.

She let me pull her in, but her red-painted lips curled in a disbelieving smirk.

"Mmm-hmm," she fussed but couldn't help the smile forming on her pretty face.

"Girl, why didn't you tell me this entrepreneur-life is ghetto?" I said as we followed the hostess to our usual booth at our favorite brunch spot, Velvet Grits.

We shared a laugh before sliding into our seats.

"Can I start you ladies with something to drink?" the hostess asked.

"Water, no ice. Mimosa flight. Shot of Tito's on the side," we replied in perfect sync.

The hostess blinked, her arched brow peaked with approval. "Coming right up."

"Sis, working for yourself will snatch your edges and your joy... for a little while at least," Sienna said, patting my hand. "But you'll find your rhythm."

"I'm exhausted but I honestly can't complain," I said, shaking my head. "I've had some great conversations with potential clients, and I feel good about what's coming. But a sista is tired and irritable. I almost snatched Sonny's head off the other day for calling me and asking about Kamryn and her damn fiancé."

"Mm-hmm... that's what happens when you get some good consistent dick then walk away from it like a fool," Sienna muttered with a knowing side-eye. "You still dreaming about that man?"

"It was one dream, SiSi." I rolled my eyes.

I was lying through my perfectly aligned teeth.

"That may be so... But you see that Mandingo of a man every night you pull out that toy." She smacked her lips and gave me a smug little tongue pop.

*The toy doesn't even do it for me after Blaize.*

Thank God the waitress came back to take our order because I couldn't say that aloud. Mostly because Sienna was right. Blaize Raymond had been stalking through my mind like a late-night infomercial—loud, persistent, and always on repeat since the moment we left Bimini.

Sienna launched into her usual routine, asking the same

questions she always did, like we hadn't eaten at Velvet Grits a thousand times. I let her charm the server while I sipped my mimosa, half-listening, half-lost in memory.

The way Blaize held me that last night... it still lingered on my skin. Those few days in paradise hadn't felt like a weekend fling. And if Blaize had his way, it wouldn't have ended there.

*"Icelyn Perry, can I see you again? When we're back? Can I take you on a real date? Not secluded in a hotel suite or hiding out at restaurants hours away from the city. I mean something **real.** I pick you up, flowers, dinner, dancing, and maybe, just maybe, a little aftercare."*

He whispered those words to me even after I said I was sure that Bimini was it for us. That's why I couldn't close that damn door. I wanted to say *yes* to everything with him.

"And for you, Miss?" The sound of the server's voice yanked me back to reality.

"Oh, um, I'll have the velvet grits and scrambled eggs with grilled chicken. A biscuit and extra whiskey maple jam, please," I replied, flashing a quick smile, though my mind was still tangled in *him.*

*Why am I torturing myself?* I didn't have time for romance. Not with a business that was still learning to walk, grown-ass kids still calling me for every little thing, and a to-do list that grew faster than my client roster. But maybe... I had time for what we *used* to have. No labels... no promises - just heat, relief, and a soft place to land when I needed it. *Girl, be for real. If you could have it every day, you would.* The truth crashed over me like cold water.

I was falling for him back then when he was young and still figuring himself out. So what made me think I could keep it casual now? Not with *this* Blaize. Not with *this* man—all fine, thick, and tender in the places that mattered. And he was patient in ways I hadn't realized I still craved.

"I have his information," Sienna crooned, tossing back her shot like it was holy water. "Cell number, email... hell, I even have an emergency contact."

"Heffa! How many times do I have to tell you no?" I groaned, rolling my eyes.

"I'm just saying... there's a solution to your problem. Why'd you tell that man no anyway? He's not young and dumb with a big dick anymore. He's grown and gainfully employed... *with* a big dick."

"I hate you so much," I muttered, smirking as I sipped my drink.

When our food arrived, we finally let it go, falling into that easy rhythm only me and my best friend could keep. Between bites and bottomless mimosas, we talked about everything and nothing for hours. The normal shenanigans: work drama, book club shade, Instagram foolishness.

Sienna paused mid-forkful and side-eyed my plate. "That's all you're gonna eat?"

I shrugged. "I haven't had much of an appetite. I've been so bloated and nauseous lately. Pretty sure my period's coming."

She raised a brow, pointing a long fuchsia nail my way. "I hope all that beach sex under the fireworks didn't result in an Independence Day baby."

I nearly choked on a bite of grits. "Girl, that's just evil... And the devil is a lie," I snorted. "Why would you even *speak* that nightmare into existence?"

Sienna cackled. "Because you and your *fire* were rekindling all kinds of flames. I know that man was blasting off in you every chance you gave him."

I shook my head, trying not to laugh. "I can't even lie... it *was* a damn sex marathon. A protected marathon...Thank you very much."

"Hmm. Even in the cabana and the shower?" she asked, lifting a brow with that all-knowing smirk.

I blinked. *Shit.* Why did I tell her every damn thing? She clocked my silence instantly.

"It only takes one time, you know." SiSi pursed her lips.

The joke soured in my gut. My stomach churned, not from food, but from *possibility*. That first night, I hadn't thought twice. I rode him wild and unthinking, sliding down on his thick, slick pole like my name was Diamond from *The Player's Club*. No protection. No hesitation. Just lust and history colliding.

"My little niece or nephew is gonna be so cute and chocolate—"

"*Stop it*, SiSi," I squealed, waving my hands like I could erase her words from the air. "I rebuke ye Satan, in the name of Jesus," I added, crossing myself like a good little heathen.

Sienna tossed her head back, amused. "I'm just saying. You've been tired, no appetite, bloated... all signs point to pregnancy, my love." She cooed like the idea was *adorable*.

I stared at my untouched plate, suddenly not so sure this feeling was *just* PMS.

------

DRIVING HOME, my head was a mess. Pregnant? At forty-eight? With two grown kids and a new business that barely let me sleep, let alone ovulate in peace? This was supposed to be the prime of my life. Booked and blessed with travel and brunches. And maybe a toxic-free dick with a side of discretion. But now? I shook my head. Janet Jackson and Da Brat had folks thinking babies after forty-five were cute. I'm here to say: that shit was a lie.

*Honk! Honk!*

I jolted back to the moment as the car behind me laid on the horn. Blinking, I checked the road, then made a sharp U-turn and pulled into the nearest drugstore parking lot. I hadn't been feeling well for at least a week. Cramps that wouldn't quit, bloating that made my jeans scream, and exhaustion so debilitating it felt like wading through cement. I'd experienced everything but a period. But I kept pushing, blaming it on stress, on starting my business, on being a woman in her forties with too much on her plate and not enough hours in the damn day.

*Of course,* I thought, grabbing a basket and pushing past a display of sweet-and-salty snacks I was craving but didn't need. *The one time my coochie finally gets her groove back, and now she's trying to snatch my whole damn uterus with it.* I hadn't needed a pregnancy test since high school and the results of that one? Oh, that bitch was positive and she now called me *Ma.*

Since I was here, I figured I might as well grab a few essentials before finally making my way to the doomsday aisle. And let me just say, whoever decided pregnancy tests, condoms, and lube should share shelf space definitely had jokes. Like, pick your path, sis… prevention, celebration, or panic.

Glancing around, I gave a polite nod to the little old couple debating which mouthwash was best for dentures. Once they shuffled off, I scanned both shoulders, then snatched three Clearblue Digitals, burying them under Twizzlers, plain Lay's, Snickers ice cream bars, and a pack of maxipads. *Wishful thinking.*

"Twenty dollars," I whispered, staring at the tag. "Highway robbery," I scoffed.

But I wasn't about to play with faint pink lines today. No guessing games, no squinting under bathroom lights. I wanted answers just as clear and easy as the label promised.

At self-checkout, I scanned my items like I was smuggling contraband. The ten-minute drive home turned into five. To my dismay, I saw Kamryn's car in the driveway. *Shit.* I didn't have the energy for another episode of Kamryn and her fiancé's bad reality TV show.

I shoved the bag into my tote and stepped out of the car, only to immediately stumble. A wave of nausea tightened my gut and knocked me sideways. I grabbed the door handle to steady myself. The cramps were getting worse. Maybe I'd been too caught up in the "am I or aren't I" spiral to notice how *bad* I actually felt. I took a deep breath in and another deep breath out, trying my best *not* to pass out in the garage.

Inside, Kamryn was already posted at the kitchen island, chewing on the last of my pineapple like she paid bills in my house.

"Hey, Ma," she said, casual as ever.

"Hey," I muttered dryly.

Her brows furrowed. "You okay?" Kamryn paused mid-bite to look at me.

I shook my head. "I don't know. I think I'm coming down with something."

*Yeah. A baby, bitch.*

"Oh, okay. Well, I need to talk to you about—"

"Kam, just... give me a minute."

I didn't wait for a reply. Instead, I made a beeline for the bathroom, but the second I shut the door, it hit me. That watery-mouth, room-spinning, cold-sweat kind of nausea that didn't care if you were too old for a baby. I dropped to my knees in front of the toilet, heaving so hard, my soul almost left my body. Something wasn't right.

"Kam!" I cried out, gripping the bowl. "Kamryn!"

"Ma?!" Her voice came closer, but it already felt far away.

The room blurred. The overhead light turned to a soft white haze. And just like that, everything went dark.

---

"Ms. Perry. Can you hear me? Can you wake up for me?"

A groan slipped from my throat as the voice called out

again, urging me back to consciousness. Why the hell was I asleep? Why did my body feel like lead, but my head floated somewhere above the clouds?

"Ms. Perry, squeeze my hand if you can hear me." That same familiar voice was gentle and sure.

I obeyed, giving the hand resting in mine the slightest squeeze. Blinking slowly, I tried to open my eyes, but the bright overhead light danced from side to side, blurring everything except the silhouette framed by its glow.

"Take your time. Go slow, Ms. Perry," the voice instructed.

And in an instant, my mind took me back to the balcony at the mansion when I straddled Blaize's lap on the outdoor lounger. The night air smoldered with heat and want as I kissed him, moaning and riding his dick like I had something to prove. His voice echoed in my ear, coarse and full of praise.

*"Damn, Ice... Take your time, baby. Go slow."*

I tried to open my eyes again but moaned aloud instead. My throat was dry and scratchy. Swallowing hard, I whispered, "Fire...Beautiful."

The broad figure bent down beside me, his full lips brushed my ear just before a low chuckle rumbled. "Yes, Madame Ice. It's your fire."

My heavy eyes popped open as wide as they could. The most beautiful sight came into view. Dark, stout, and glorious.

"Jesus," I croaked groggily.

"I've been called worse," he teased, stepping closer.

"Though if I remember right, the last time you called for Jesus, I had just—"

That baritone. That nickname. That confirmation. It was *him*. Instead of relief spreading over me, I panicked. My body jerked upright only to be slammed back down by a searing pain in my lower belly.

"Hey... easy, easy," he urged. "Ice, please stay calm," he continued, holding my hand in his while the other massaged my temple. "You're at St. Gabriel Hospital. You had surgery."

The blur sharpened and there he was. *Blaize. Motherfucking. Raymond.*

"Surgery? Hospital? What are you doing here? Did I lose the baby?" The words tumbled out before I could stop them.

His eyes were wide but soft at the same time. "I work here, Icelyn. And... there was no baby, sweetheart."

Relief washed over me like a crashing wave. "Oh, thank God." I exhaled deeply, resting my head back. "Wait... are you a doctor? My... doctor?"

He shook his head, that slow, sexy grin playing on his lips. "I'm your nurse."

*Shit.*

# *blaize*

What were the odds that Icelyn Perry—*Madame Ice herself*—would be admitted to the hospital on the exact night I picked up a shift for a coworker who called out sick? Blyss was still with her mom for another week, so I had no real excuse to say no to the extra hours. It was either overtime or another night losing to the PlayStation while nursing a few too many Coronas.

I'd just clocked in when the red light started blinking. An ambulance was inbound. Nothing I needed to rush for unless I was officially paged. As a CRNA, I was typically only called in to support the anesthesiologist during surgery.

After tossing my bag in the locker and grabbing my water bottle, I headed to the nurse's station to see what the night had in store. Broken arms, chest pains, and dehydration were a typical night in the ER. Contrary to every medical drama on

TV, the emergency room wasn't all adrenaline and chaos. Most nights were routine—broken bones, bad decisions, and the occasional gunshot wound or a fed-up wife who finally snapped.

Then my pager buzzed.

PAGE: [OR-3. Surgical Prep.]
Female, 48, Acute Pelvic Pain,
Possible ectopic

*Shit.* My night changed just that fast. I scrubbed in quickly, mind already switching to surgical mode. Time was of the essence in a potential ectopic pregnancy. One wrong move, or too much delay, and we'd be looking at internal bleeding or worse.

As the lead nurse rattled off vitals—*BP 145 over 90, no chronic conditions, no significant history*—I nodded along, my focus narrowing in. These details were critical. One miscalculated dose, or a misjudged response, and things could go south real quick.

I rounded the surgical table, casually glancing at the woman already under light sedation, and then my breath caught. *Icelyn.* Even groggy, she was unforgettable.

Her honey-brown skin was streaked with dried tears, and her full lips were slightly parted as if mid-thought. The braids from vacation were gone, replaced with soft curls that fanned around the pillow like a halo. I froze. Just for a second, but long enough for the weight of the moment to settle deep in my chest.

"Nurse Raymond." The sound of my name snapped me out of it.

I blinked and looked up at my colleague, nodding quickly. "Got it—BP 145 over 90, no chronic conditions, no significant history," I said, steadying my voice just enough to sound like I was fully present. Even if my heart was still catching up.

*Is she pregnant? Losing the baby? My... baby?*

Icelyn wasn't fully under, still conscious enough to feel. Her body tensed, and a strained breath slipped through trembling lips as she grimaced. I adjusted the anesthesia carefully, watching her chest rise unevenly.

My face was hidden behind a mask, and I prayed she wouldn't recognize me... at least not yet. This wasn't how I ever imagined seeing her again. Not like this: In a thin hospital gown. In pain. And definitely not with her fate, quite literally, resting in my hands. But my job didn't ask for permission so here we were.

"Can you count to ten for me, Ms. Perry?" I asked, eyes flicking from her face to the monitors. My voice was calm and professional, but inside, I felt every second stretch too long.

She gave me the slightest nod, lips parting sluggishly. "One... two... three... four..." Her words slurred, volume trailing off as her lashes fluttered, heavy against her cheeks. By the time she reached five, her breathing had evened, her body sinking deeper into the table.

Three hours later, Icelyn was out of surgery and resting

in her room. Thankfully, the procedure had gone smoothly. No complications and no baby. That last part hit me harder than I thought it would. My chest tightened with something between guilt and relief. She didn't need that kind of stress. Hell, neither of us did.

Having more kids was something I used to toss around back when my ex and I were still trying to force something that had already fallen apart. But now? In a moment like this? A situation I couldn't fully comprehend, let alone explain? It would've been a damn disaster.

It was four in the morning and the hospital hallways had quieted. Nurses moved like shadows, carts rolling softly over polished floors. I finished my shift over an hour ago, but I couldn't leave. Not without seeing her.

Room 618.

I slipped in without turning on the light, just letting the moonlight leak through the window blinds and cast a soft glow over her body. She was curled slightly to the side, IV hooked to her arm, and her lips parted slightly. *Fucking beautiful.*

The sky was shifting in that in-between hour when the world was quietly holding its breath. Her daughter and Sienna had been there for hours - waiting, watching, and praying. But when she still hadn't come to, they were advised to leave and get some rest. I kept my distance because I didn't want her friend to see me—not before Icelyn.

I sat in the corner of her room, elbows on my knees,

fingers laced tight. My scrubs were wrinkled and my badge hung crooked. I was exhausted. I'd forgotten to eat, and the vending machine coffee was trash, but I held my eyes open long enough to stick around for her.

After Icelyn's surgery, another page came through, making it a busier night than I was prepared to handle. I'd seen several patients wheeled into recovery, monitored vitals, and held shaking hands of panicked family members. But she wasn't just any patient. This was *her*.

Icelyn was the woman partially responsible for the man I'd become. Back when we were each other's confidants, she was the one who encouraged me to find my own way. To want more than just a rotating badge number and a *companion* to women.

When my father probably would've preferred I become a doctor, I chose something different. I didn't want distance. I wanted presence. Something that would allow me a different kind of relationship with patients. And she pushed me to follow that instinct... even when I doubted myself.

I rubbed a hand over my beard, trying to find a second wind, when I noticed her stir. Her brow twitched and lashes fluttered like she was fighting her way through a fog. I sat up straighter in the chair beside her bed, placing the chart I hadn't really been reading on the side table.

"Hey," I said gently, leaning forward. "You're okay, Ice. You're okay."

She blinked, slow and disoriented, mouth open with a shallow breath. Her eyes searched until they found mine. They were blurry at first, then suddenly locked in, like gravity had a hold on both of us. Her fingers twitched under the blanket.

"Fire?" she rasped.

My chest tightened, but I smiled anyway. "I'm here."

Her eyes widened, confusion flashing in them, then recognition. Panic. She clearly didn't remember our moment right after surgery.

"You're my... nurse?" she asked, her voice rough but curious, like something was tugging at the edge of her memory.

The question told me she recalled just enough to know I'd been there.

"Technically, yeah," I said, keeping my tone light. "Certified Registered Nurse Anesthetist. I was covering the night shift when you came in." I tried to smile again. "My job's to keep you asleep when we need you to be... and make sure you wake up when it matters." I chuckled, but my voice caught slightly at the end.

Her forehead wrinkled as she tried to sit up. "What... happened to me?"

I didn't answer right away. "What's the last thing you remember?"

She blinked slowly, her head shifting just enough to suggest pain. "Um... brunch with SiSi. Pregnancy tests. Kam was at my house." Her voice cracked. "I remember the pain. Sharp... in my stomach. Then I screamed..." Her brows drew together. "And then nothing. Now you."

I stood and adjusted the bed, easing her back against the pillows. "You had a ruptured fibroid," I said, softening my tone. "It caused internal bleeding. We had to perform an emergency hysterectomy. You lost a lot of blood, Ice. It was serious."

She didn't respond, just stared at the ceiling, trying to make sense of it all. Then she turned back toward me, eyes now glassy. "They took everything?" she said, not a statement, but a question.

I nodded slowly, sitting on the edge of the bed beside her. "Yeah. It was the only way to stop the bleeding and keep you safe."

She swallowed hard, her throat working against the lump lodged there. A single tear slid free, trailing back onto the pillow as she whispered, "I'm sorry." Her eyes darted away, shame flickering across them. "It's so stupid to cry," she muttered, voice catching. Then she forced out a humorless laugh. "My old ass didn't need any more babies anyway."

I reached for her hand, closing the already small space between us. Leaning in, I held her gaze. "Nah," I murmured. "You can feel this, Ice. This can hurt. It's okay."

Her lashes fluttered fast, trying and failing, to blink it back. Then the dam broke. Her hands, wrapped in tape and IV lines, came up to cover her face as the wail escaped her throat.

I pressed my lips gently to her temple. "I won't pretend to understand everything you're feeling right now," I whispered. "But I do know this... you're still you." I kissed her forehead and brushed the tears from her cheeks. "The strongest, baddest, most unforgettable woman I've ever met."

She squeezed my hand. "They took the part of me that made me a woman."

I opened my mouth, but she kept going, her words tumbling out like loose bricks from a collapsing wall.

"I know... I know I've had my children. I should be grateful... I *am* grateful because this could've been worse. But I didn't get to *choose* this. I didn't get to say when I was done." She exhaled shakily. "And now it's just... gone." That last word lingered in the air, fading with the moon as it slipped away, making room for morning light.

We sat in silence until it shifted from uncomfortable to healing. Her eyes, still red from crying, held the weight of everything she'd just endured. But the faint smile tugging at her lips told me she'd be okay. Maybe not right away, but eventually she'd find her way back.

I knew we couldn't stay like this much longer. The morning nurse would be in soon to check her vitals, and I had officially crossed the line from exhaustion into delirium.

"I can't believe this is real," she whispered.

"Give yourself some time, Ice," I said, sitting up. "To heal. Not just physically... completely."

She shook her head. "No. I mean you being here. Last night, when everything happened. What are the odds? First Bimini... now me, in the hospital where you work?"

I nodded slowly. "On the night I wasn't even scheduled to be here," I said, chuckling. "Fate's got a fucked-up sense of humor."

Her eyes drifted to my name badge, then to the stethoscope slung around my neck.

"So you're *Nurse* Fire now? With a degree, 401(k), and direct deposit?" she teased, a small smirk pulling at her lips.

I grinned. "And your Lord and Savior, apparently. Don't forget that part—*Jesus*," I said, mimicking her voice from earlier.

She let out a soft laugh, then winced. "Ugh. Don't make me laugh. That hurts."

"I got you." I pressed the button to recline the bed just slightly. As she shifted, I adjusted the blanket over her shoulders, tucking it in with care.

My fingers brushed against her skin. She was just as warm and soft as I remembered. My hands lingered a breath longer than they should have before she settled back into the pillows.

The sudden beep pulled our attention to the monitor. Her heart rate was climbing, the numbers ticking upward with every gentle stroke. She looked at me, her pretty eyes heavy with want... and what's next. I stared back, unable to stop touching her. Shit, I wanted to feel her everywhere.

"You should rest," I murmured, tapping the tip of her nose before taking a small step back.

"I should," she echoed.

But her eyes didn't close. She just kept watching me, like if she blinked, I might disappear. I didn't move either. I sat there, letting the silence speak for us.

And in that stillness, it was clear... we were standing on the edge of something we pretended not to see, but the universe was deciding for us. Because that old flame? Yeah, it was still burning. And this time, I wasn't letting it burn out.

"Good night, Madame Ice," I whispered, brushing a stray curl from her cheek.

Then I kissed her softly three times like a promise. Or maybe... I miss you. I want you. Maybe even... I love you. She closed her eyes as my fingertips traced gently down her face. And finally, she drifted to sleep.

# *icelyn*

"Shit," I groaned, lifting from the couch like my bones were made of splintered glass.

The day had been drenched in gray. Heavy clouds hung low, swallowing the sky whole. Rain had tapped against the window like a slow lullaby, pulling me in and out of sleep. It had been a week since I got home from the hospital, and I was already doing way more than the doctor ordered.

Moving like a damn sloth, I crept toward the door as the bell rang again. Louder this time. Like whoever was on the other side was trying to wake the dead. My lovely daughter, who was *supposed* to be my caretaker, had left over an hour ago to "grab something from the store." She knew good and well I wasn't supposed to be on my feet unless absolutely necessary.

"I'm coming!" I yelled, annoyed and aching.

I gripped the wall, steadying myself as I tiptoed like a baby deer on black ice. They'd just have to wait until I got there. But whoever this was... was about to get cursed out. Real good, too.

When I finally cracked the door open, ready to give somebody a piece of my mind,

my mouth fell open instead. *Blaize.* Tall and fine as ever in a charcoal-gray T-shirt and joggers. His clothes matched the dreary day, but like divine timing, a soft beam of sunlight broke through the clouds the moment I saw him.

He held a bouquet of yellow tulips and red roses in one hand and a plastic bag from Harlan's Deli in the other. *Two of my favorite things.* When we were in our situationship, if I'd had a rough week filled with gaslighting colleagues and micro-aggressive meetings, he'd show up at the hotel suite with the room draped in flowers and my favorite meal already on the table.

"Blaize?"

"Why are you up, Ice?" he asked, head tilted like he already knew I was breaking the rules.

His eyes swept over me. Hair in a nappy puff, blue mumu hanging off my sore body, and exhaustion etched all over my face, yet still, they softened with something that looked an awful lot like admiration.

"What are you doing here?" I asked, confused and completely caught off guard.

"Checking on my patient," he said with a grin. "May I?" He nodded toward the inside of the house, waiting for permission to enter.

I couldn't help but laugh. "I didn't know you made house calls," I said, stepping aside.

"Only for my special patients." He winked.

Before I could respond, his gentle arm slid around my waist, perfectly supporting me like he knew exactly where I was hurting. He walked me to the couch like it was the most natural thing in the world, helping me lower myself onto the cushions with care.

"You here alone?" he asked, scanning the room.

I nodded. "My *wonderful* daughter was supposed to pick up my meds and grab food. That was over an hour ago."

He raised a brow and set the deli bag and flowers on the coffee table. "Well, good thing I came prepared."

I blinked back the sudden emotion rising in my throat. He wasn't supposed to be here. Not in my house. Not with that voice. Not with those hands. And definitely not with that familiar scent wrapping around my ribs like the best damn cuddler I ever had.

Blaize Raymond had no business showing up, reminding me of everything I want and everything we could never be... All at the same time. But damn, the comfort he brought with him settled in deeper than the strongest pain meds I had.

I watched him move through my space like he'd been there before. He unwrapped the sandwich, removed the lid from the soup, then set everything, along with a bottle of water, on the tray beside the couch. My eyes flicked to the familiar brown paper bag, stained with spots of oil from the Italian beef.

"You remembered," I gushed.

"I remember everything, Ice," he replied, cracking open the bottle and handing it to me.

I took a sip, and right on cue, sparks flared the moment our fingers brushed. He leaned over me then, adjusting the pillows with quiet precision. My questioning eyes followed his every movement. I had to fight the urge to do something stupid like bury my face in his chest just to breathe him in.

He smelled unfair, like your favorite sugary dessert while on the keto diet... and I craved a taste. And those gray sweatpants weren't helping. There was no concealing what he was working with, but in gray damn sweatpants? My eyes saw everything and my body noticed before my brain could tell it to behave.

Gently, he propped up my feet in the perfect position like he knew exactly how to care for me. Like he *wanted* to take care of me.

"Blaize..." I said, my voice quieter now. "Why are you *really* here? How did you know where I live?"

He lifted my feet to sit beside me on the couch, then rested my feet in his lap. Aimlessly massaging them, his eyes never left mine.

"Well, I got your address from your patient record," he said, shrugging.

I shook my head. "Stalking ass," I teased, scooping up a spoonful of tortellini soup.

He snickered. "And I'm here because I couldn't stop thinking about you since you left that hospital. You had me worried... I'm still worried." He shifted closer, voice lower now. "How are you, really, Icelyn?"

My eyes flicked to his, then dropped just as fast, landing on a piece of lint clinging to my dress. I sucked in a dragging breath, appetite fading under the weight of the past few weeks. I stayed in the hospital longer than expected because of a blood clot.

And even now, back home, I didn't feel like myself. I felt... hollow. Like something inside had been taken out and the space left behind was still echoing. But nobody seemed to notice the tiredness that sleep couldn't fix and the ache that wasn't just from stitches or surgical scars. Nobody except *him* had asked.

"I just..." I cleared my throat. "Thank you. For staying with me. I don't remember much, but I remember you being there."

Every night, after hours, in the midst of darkness and often loneliness, Blaize would appear like a thief in the night. The only difference was he wasn't stealing anything, he was bringing joy. Some nights I was so heavily medicated that I couldn't open my eyes long enough to notice who was in the room, but I could hear him... *feel* him.

"You don't have to thank me," he spoke softly. Then he bent forward and pressed a kiss to the top of my foot.

"I do," I said, voice thin bordering on a whine. "I was scared. Confused. And you made me feel safe." I paused, trying to smile past the lump forming in my throat. "But didn't you have anything better to do than babysit me?" I joked, hoping to lift the heaviness.

"Not when my Madame Icey's in recovery," he said, that smooth grin sliding across his face.

I laughed and instantly winced. "God. Everything still hurts."

"You've gotta take it easy. Rest," he urged softly. "Just rest, sweetheart."

And for the first time in days, I felt like I actually could. I leaned back, eyes fluttering closed as the steady tap of rain intensified against the window. A hush settled over us - full but not uncomfortable.

"Kamryn told me she thought I died for a minute," I whispered. "Said I was pale and cold and she couldn't wake me up. I've never seen my baby cry like that."

Blaize didn't respond right away. Instead, his hand moved slowly up and down my leg, in featherlight, comforting strokes.

"You didn't die, Ice." He paused, and when he spoke again, the usual ease was gone from his voice. "But you were in bad shape when they brought you in. It scared the hell out of me when I saw you like that."

I opened my eyes and met his gaze. There was no teasing now. No smirk. No clever comeback. Just concern. And something deeper I couldn't quite identify. I looked away, my jaw tightening against the wave rising in my chest.

"Can I ask you something?" he said quietly.

I nodded, already bracing.

He hesitated. "Why didn't you tell anyone you'd been feeling off? The extent of it. You had to have pain. Bloating. Maybe even bleeding..."

I shrugged, my gaze falling to the blanket he'd tucked around me earlier.

"I thought it was stress. Hormones. Just life stacking up, you know?" My voice thinned. "I was being another Black woman pushing through it all. Ignoring the signs. Convincing myself it wasn't that bad."

A dry laugh escaped me. "Hell, SiSi had me thinking I was pregnant."

He exhaled sharply through his nose and shook his head. "You scared the hell out of me, Ice." The tremble in his bass couldn't be denied.

"You keep saying that," I murmured, my voice barely above a whisper. "But why? Why were you scared?"

His eyes snapped to mine. "Because it's *you*, Icelyn. You weren't just another patient."

"Who am I then, Blaize?" I shot back.

He didn't answer right away. Instead, his hand, still resting beneath the blanket, moved slowly, tracing absent patterns along my thigh. My breath hitched, not from the contact alone, but from the weight of whatever he was about to say.

Blaize leaned his head back against the couch, eyes fixed on the ceiling as if gathering courage.

"You were my person, Icelyn Perry," he admitted quietly, then looked at me. "The one who got away... twice. And *seeing* you like that..." He swallowed, shaking his head. "I didn't know if I'd get another chance to say that out loud."

His words, paired with the steady glide of his hand along my leg, sent warmth unfolding low in my belly. My head eased back against the pillow, my eyes lowering in quiet surrender. A soft sigh slipped from my lips as I shifted beneath his touch. Not from pain this time, but from something deeper.

"Blaize," I breathed.

This wasn't just want. It was everything I'd been trying *not* to feel since the moment he walked through my front door. Since that kiss on the beach when I knew without hesitation he was still my fire. If I'm honest with myself, those feelings didn't start there. I'd just buried them the day we walked away from each other years ago.

The tension clinging to me—emotional and otherwise—started to loosen under his hands. But I couldn't let myself get swept away. Not completely. I needed to stay realistic. Yes, he was older and wiser now. Yes, he'd built a better life for himself. But Blaize was still eight years younger than me.

That had been fine back then when he was just my little secret. My escape. My hideaway. But the look in his eyes now? This man didn't want to be hidden. He wanted the world to know I was his and he was mine.

"You know this can't go anywhere," I whispered.

"I don't know that at all," he replied without flinching.

"I know what you're telling yourself. But I also know the way you looked at me every night in that hospital room. The way you squeezed my hand even when you were so medicated you could barely keep your eyes open but you still knew it was me." He lifted a brow, daring me to deny it. "And I remember exactly how we felt in Bimini. I remember *us*... all those years ago."

I bit my lip, unable to argue. His receipts were valid.

He slid his hands down to the soles of my feet, kneading

with firm, practiced pressure, yet still impossibly gentle. When he lifted one foot and pressed a kiss to my toes, the warmth of his mouth made my breath stall. There was nothing rushed in his movements. No performance or urgency. This wasn't seduction. It was adoration.

"Let me take care of you, Madame Ice," he whispered. "Just for now. We'll figure out the details later. But know this…" He reached up, gently nudging my chin so I had no choice but to look at him. "…I'm not going anywhere."

Before I could argue, his mouth trailed tepid, lingering kisses along my toes, and I nearly came undone. His palm skimmed up the curve of my thigh, stopping just shy of where I ached most. He knew the doctor's orders—no sex for six weeks, nothing that could strain the healing incision.

But his touch? It wasn't just about desire. Don't get me wrong, I wished he could climb up here and fuck the shit out of me, dismantling every ounce of restraint I had left. But this… this was sacred. It always had been. Not just the release. Not just the comfort. The connection. What he once called… aftercare.

"Can I take care of you, Ice?" he asked again, his voice laced with unwavering patience.

I nodded, sinking deeper into the couch as his hands moved with quiet devotion, drawing soft, involuntary breaths from my lips. I closed my eyes for a second, just long enough to savor it. Like if I labored too long, the moment might disappear.

When I opened them again, I forced a little humor back into my voice. "So what now? You just gonna keep popping up like a fine-ass guardian angel?" I bit my bottom lip, failing to hide the grin tugging at it.

That gorgeous crooked smile curved across his beautiful face. "Is that what you want?"

I smirked, despite myself. "Maybe."

# blaize

Icelyn had drifted off with her head on my shoulder, the soft rise and fall of her breath brushing against my collarbone. Her body was finally relaxed, and I didn't dare move, not with the way she fit there. Not with how natural it felt to hold her again.

A sound broke the quiet. The metallic creak of a door. Maybe the garage. A moment later came the rustle of plastic and soft footsteps across the kitchen tile.

"Ma?" a voice called. "I'm so sorry. I know I took forever. David needed me to drop something off at the house."

The voice was still talking as the person stepped into the living room, two bags swinging from her arms. Then she stopped. Her eyes landed on me... *on us*. Confusion flickered, narrowing her gaze as she tried to connect the dots. I didn't move, just gave a respectful and unapologetic nod.

"Um... who are you?" Kamryn asked, brows pulling tight.

Icelyn stirred at her daughter's voice, forehead creased before her eyes blinked open.

"Kamryn?" she said, tone thick from sleep.

Concern softened her daughter's face instantly. "Yeah, Ma. I'm here. I'm sorry. It took way longer than I thought. Dave had to—"

"Where the hell have you been?" Icelyn snapped, wincing as she tried to sit straighter. "You've been gone for..." She glanced at the clock handing on the wall. "Three hours, Kamryn. Three. I told you I wasn't supposed to be alone." Her voice cracked as she pressed a hand to her side. "I need my medication."

"I know, Ma," Kamryn said quickly, guilt spreading across her face. "I know. I'm sorry. I thought you'd sleep while I was—"

"Well, I didn't," Icelyn cut in. "And now everything fucking hurts again."

I laid a hand on her shoulder. "Ice, breathe. Don't strain yourself."

Sucking in a rough inhale, she nodded but kept her eyes locked on her daughter. Emotional hurt mingled with the physical pain that lingered behind the anger like asking for help had turned into another wound.

"Seems like you're doing alright to me," Kamryn mumbled breathily, but her mother's glare shut her down. "Sorry," she whispered. "Um, who are you?" she asked again.

"I'm Blaize," I said, rising slowly to shake her hand. "A friend."

Kamryn opened her mouth, but Icelyn cut her off. "Just give me my medicine, put the groceries away, and go."

"Ma, I'm—"

"Sorry," Icelyn snapped, cutting Kamryn off. "Yeah, you said that already."

Ice snatched the pharmacy bag from her daughter's extended hand, ripping open the package to retrieve the medication. Angrily, she tossed the pills into her mouth, gulping the water down.

"Ma, please," Kamryn whined, tears filling her matching brown eyes.

"If David's the priority, then go on and handle that. I'll manage. I'm good." Icelyn rolled her eyes, heat sharp as glass.

Kamryn eyed her mother before huffing, then stomping toward the kitchen. Icelyn's eyes pooled but she blinked back the impending tears, refusing to let them fall. She didn't want to talk about it. I could see that clear as day. So I did what I did best—slid closer, laid a hand on her shoulder, and just... cared for her.

"Try to eat a little more since you've taken the medicine," I requested.

She nodded, unwrapping the sandwich from earlier and forcing a few bites. Kamryn reappeared moments later. I honestly thought she'd left.

"Ma, let me help you to bed," she said, her tone soft, almost childlike.

"Kam, I said I'm fine. You can go."

The tension snapped sharp in the air, and my first

instinct was to leave since this was family business. Icelyn looked like she was a whooping mama who didn't care one bit that her daughter was grown.

The rage in her eyes said Kamryn was two seconds away from being sent outside to pick a switch. But before I could stand from the couch, Icelyn's hand shot out and wrapped around my wrist.

"Kam. Go," she said firmly, eyes pinched tight. "We'll talk tomorrow when I've calmed down."

Then her gaze softened as it cut to me. "You... stay."

Shit... I did what I was told and sat my ass down.

# icelyn

I had no idea what I was doing asking him to stay. The only thing I knew for certain was that I wanted him here. *Needed* him here. Maybe Blaize was right. Maybe the universe really didn't make mistakes. I didn't know where this was going, but I knew I wanted him beside me.

"You ready?" His voice pulled my gaze up.

We'd moved to my bedroom. He was still in those damn gray sweatpants, but now in a black tank that clung to his chest, ink curling over muscles I'd traced with my tongue too many times to count. Time had only sharpened him, sweetened the treasure that was *him*.

He'd aged like a priceless wine, but at his core, he was still the fine-ass, chiseled-ass, hypnotic-dick-ass young man with the heart of gold. Even the first time I saw him when my daughter was fighting to breathe, I noticed him. Of course I did. How could I not?

I shook my head. "I can't take a bath yet. You should know that, Nurse Raymond," I teased, perched on the edge of the chair.

He smirked. "I'm aware. But there are other ways to get you clean, Icelyn." His eyes softened as he stepped closer, hand extended. "May I?" he asked, motioning toward my mumu.

Something in his thoughtful tone made my belly rumble. I nodded. He lifted the fabric slowly, careful not to tug at my incisions.

"Easy," he whispered when I flinched.

His hands steadied me when I pressed against the compression garment across my stomach. My breasts ached, hypersensitive even to the brush of his fingertips. The way he moved, so patient, so present, felt like its own kind of medicine.

When he slid my panties down, he braced me, letting me lean on to his shoulder as I stepped out. His palm rested at the small of my back, his other hand hovering protectively at my stomach.

Step by step, he guided me to the bed, unfolding a towel across the mattress before helping me climb onto it. He tucked the blanket over me like I was something precious, then disappeared into the bathroom.

A few minutes later, he returned with a gray basin of soapy water with a towel draped over his shoulder. His eyes were colored with compassionate and that always brought me peace. Every time he was in my presence, I couldn't control my eyes. They moved with him, following his every thoughtful and deliberate step.

The lights were already dimmed, and the rain outside, now lighter, drummed against the windows, the perfect soundtrack for what Blaize did best... care. He moved stealthily, perusing my body like a skilled artist studying his canvas. Or maybe like the nurse he was, preparing to deliver the exact dose of medicine I didn't know I needed.

I sucked in a breath when the heated towel hit my stomach, easing the tension near the incisions. Exhaling, my head eased against the pillow, surrendering to the abyss called *Blaize*. He took another towel, washing my feet before gliding the warm cloth up my right leg, then the left.

"Does that feel good?" he asked but continued speaking before I could answer. "The heat helps your blood flow. Helps relieve a bit of the pain."

"Mmhmm," was all I could muster.

He was still talking but all I could pay attention to was the way his deep voice wrapped around me almost as hot as his touch. A tremble coursed through me in anticipation of his next stop on his canvas that we me. He approached the slick folds of my pussy with meticulous attention.

Damn the hot towel because my essence was already on fire for him. Thick lips kissed my private lips like it the was the most natural thing to do. Then another soft kiss as if he was simply saying good morning. And then another just a sweet as leisurely as the ones before.

Every instinct told my hips to buck, to chase the pleasure, but the pain would've dropped me. So I let a deep, guttural moan spill out instead.

"Aaah."

"Did you know-" he said casually like he wasn't currently tongue-deep in my sanity. "-that orgasms have healing effects?" he asked, voice vibrating against my swollen center.

I shook my head, unable to craft a coherent sentence.

"Mmm-hmm. They release endorphins and oxytocin, which can alleviate pain, loosen tension, and calm your nervous system." His tongue flicked over me as he spoke, and the knowledge hit almost as hard as the satisfaction. "So this isn't just for you to feel good. It's for you to *get better*."

This time, a slow kiss... then a host of them along my inner thigh. He lifted his eyes to mine, his voice steady — grounding me.

"Right now, your scar tissue is tight," he murmured. "But pleasure... an orgasm..." His tongue flattened, dragging a path that made me gasp. "It teaches the body to relax."

Another lick. This time slow and lazy. His mouth continued its patient path. The sensation made my breath stagger. Heat gathered low, building not in frenzy, but in awareness. I couldn't calm my breathing. I wanted this. Needed it.

"Look at me, Ice," he said softly.

I heard him, but my body was too far gone to respond. My mind lagged behind the feeling.

He paused the lascivious attack on my pussy, lifting his head. "Baby... look at me." He emphasized each word.

Slowly but surely, my eyes opened and found his. He hovered above me now, pressing gentle kisses along the curve between my breasts.

"Ice," he said evenly. "Your body may be changing… but it's still yours, sweetheart. It's still whole. And it's still worthy of being satisfied."

"Blaize…" I moaned.

My tears didn't have time to gather. They slipped free without warning. I fisted the sheets, an unimaginable sensation rippled through me. Not just physical, but emotional, and he wasn't even touching me.

My overwhelm had nothing to do with urgency and everything to do with being *seen*. With being reminded. And for the first time since the surgery — maybe even for the first time in years — I didn't feel broken.

"Blaize," I moaned again softly, and he knew exactly what I needed without another word.

"I got you, beautiful."

My head tossed back, burrowed in the pillow as soon as he slid his tongue inside me. The motion was unhurried and controlled to ensure I could take it. I wanted him to go faster, deeper. Shit, I desired more than his tongue, but of course, we couldn't. *Fucking six week wait.*

"This pressure?" he said, momentarily pausing his pursuit. "That's to wake your pelvic floor. Remind your body it's alive. That it can still *want*. Still *feel*," he whispered, guiding that snake he called a tongue back in me.

The rhythm built but wasn't rushed, nor greedy. It was measured and intentional, like he was pacing my healing as much as my fulfillment. His free hand pressed gently to my hips, holding me still.

"Blaize. Shit. Oh my God," I moaned, gripping the sides

of his head. "I want you. I need you." My voice cracked, tears prickling at my lashes.

He shook his head slowly, eyes locked on mine. "I know you want this dick, but that's not happening. Not yet, baby."

The denial gutted me. A sob broke free. "You feel so good..."

"Mmm-hmm," he hummed against me, agreeing with his mouth as much as his words.

"Why are you doing this to me?" I begged.

He kissed me again, then lifted his head just enough to speak. "You know why this feels so damn good?"

I could only whimper, lost in the euphoria stealing my common sense. His lips curved in wicked patience.

"Because the tongue is nothing but muscle and nerves. Strong, yet sensitive. Built to taste, to tease, to learn." He gave a long, deliberate stroke that left me shaking. "And right now, Ice, all it's learning is *you*."

A single tear slid down my cheek because this nigga was really talking me through my orgasm. Narrating every moment like my body was a story only he knew how to read. His voice was coaxing and relentless, wrapping around me like the sweetest caress.

"B... Blaize—" My voice broke, trembling like my body. My fingers gripped his head tighter, desperate and undone.

"Breathe with me," he cut in, his tone was soft but commanding. "In through your nose. Let it out through your mouth."

I obliged and he rewarded me with a comforting, "Good girl."

The orgasm crept like a tide, then crashed, rolling through me until my vision blurred. Every nerve ending, every muscle ached with the release, but the scar's pull, the ache that had owned me, dulled into something faint. Like background noise under a symphony of pleasure.

Blaize kissed the inside of my thigh. "See? Medicine." He looked up at me, smiling that quiet smile that always made me weak. "Better than pills, wouldn't you agree?"

I laughed breathlessly, happy tears slipping from the corners of my eyes. "So much better."

My body had felt like foreign territory for weeks. Patched up and abandoned. But in that climactic rush, that wave crashing over me, I remembered I was still here. I could still feel, still experience pleasure. Stitched and tender, yes—but still beautiful. Still mine.

*Who was I kidding? This body belonged to him.*

TWENTY-THREE

*blaize*

It was Friday. My favorite day of the week because I got to see my Madame Ice. But this Friday felt different. The energy between us was off. It had been for a couple of weekends now. Like we both already knew the end was loitering in the room, waiting for one of us to say it out loud.

As always, I was the first to arrive to the hotel. Icelyn came into the suite the same way she always did—soft knock, keycard slide, that faint hint of warm peaches and vanilla trailing in behind her. I sat by the window with a glass of dark liquor, watching the city lights flicker on as day gave way to night.

I'd already completed the tasks meant to please Madame Ice. Select my favorite sexy lingerie and have it ready for her to change into when she arrived. Check.

The black lace shorts and matching crop tank were laid out across the bed, waiting for her to fill them with that thick frame I knew by heart.

*Order one of her favorite meals and make it a good surprise. Check.*

*Dinner waited beneath a silver cover—salmon with crab cream sauce, cheese ravioli, broccoli, and a Caesar salad, no croutons, extra dressing.*

*I knew her preferences to a tee, and I followed them meticulously. Yes, it was my job, but more importantly, it was what I wanted to do. Only for her.*

*You'd think a routine like ours would grow stale. But the faint blush blooming across her cheeks told me she still felt seen. Still felt cared for. I wished that would be enough to keep us from falling apart. But it wasn't.*

*Ice moved slower than usual, her eyes scanning the room like it was unfamiliar. Like she'd never been here before. But the suite hadn't changed. It was the same room we'd escaped to every other weekend.*

*Sleek gold lamps glowing softly beside polished wood tables. A plush king-sized bed dressed in crisp white linens. A small sitting area with a charcoal-gray loveseat tucked near the window.*

*Everything was exactly as it had always been. Except her.*

*"Hey," she murmured timidly.*

*Icelyn Perry... timid? Never. That should've been my first warning we were already done. I didn't turn around. I couldn't.*

*"You're late," I said, voice flat, eyes locked on the window because looking at her would've broken me.*

*"Work was a beast today. Same old shit, but for some reason today was..." Her voice drifted off.*

*"Tough," I finished.*

*She nodded.*

*I understood. Today had been rough for me, too. Everything that could go wrong did, almost like the universe was preparing us for broken hearts. Or maybe just me.*

*I lifted the glass to my lips but didn't drink, watching her reflection in it instead. She hadn't moved from the center of the room, like her feet were fused to the tan carpet. Like the memories weren't quite landing where they used to.*

*Or maybe she was absorbing them... swallowing each one for safekeeping in her heart. But honestly, she looked like she wanted to disappear. Be anywhere but here.*

*"Are you staying, Icelyn?" I asked, cutting straight through it.*

*"What?" she said with a hint of annoyance, clutching her bag tighter while she still standing in the middle of the room.*

*"By now, you'd be out of those clothes and on my lap, telling me about your day while I fed you," I said, my voice laced with something teetering toward torment.*

*"I don't know." She shrugged, her tone softer than I'd ever heard.*

*"You don't know what?" My jaw tightened. "Whether you're staying with me?"*

*She nodded.*

*I shook my head. "Stop, Ice." I exhaled hard. "Just... stop. I already know."*

*Her body stayed frozen in place, but somehow I still felt the shift in her breath from across the room.*

*Our contract was supposed to end today. What she didn't know was that I'd ended it months ago. Icelyn wasn't a job anymore. She was a woman I wanted to take care of. Love.*

*I just wasn't ready. And my life—so unfinished and unsettled —wasn't what she needed in hers.*

*"Ray," she whispered. "This... this has gone too far." Her voice cracked on the last word. The same voice that had whispered, "I think I love you," into my mouth just last week.*

*I swallowed hard, staring into my glass like it might tell me how to survive this. My throat burned as I nodded and said, "I know."*

*I pushed back from the chair, the scrape loud in the quiet, and finally turned to face her.*

*"I was up all damn night," I said, stepping closer. "Trying to figure out how to get my shit together. What I needed to fix. How to keep you. How to be enough."*

*She reached for me, cradling my face in her hand, those dewy honey-colored eyes holding mine.*

*"You are an amazing man," she said softly. "And some woman is going to be blessed to have you in her life."*

The car alarm blaring outside the window jolted me from the memory. Since seeing Icelyn in Bimini, our last night together had been lodged in my head, skipping in the same place like a scratched record I couldn't lift the needle from.

It was all true. I hadn't had my shit together back then. I was young, dumb, working as an EMT and a damn escort.

There were so many moments after that infamous Friday night when I wanted to call her. Hell, I wanted to find her and make her mine. But I was man enough to admit I didn't have anything to offer her then, and Icelyn deserved the world. She deserved the man I was today.

A soft throat-clearing followed by a quiet wince pulled

my focus from the window to the bed. A glance at the clock on the nightstand told me it was nearly ten in the morning. She had to be hurting since she'd gone without pain meds for almost twelve hours.

"Good morning," I said, crossing the room. I placed two pills in her palm and a bottle of water in the other. "Drink some fluids, then take your meds."

A groggy smile greeted me as I sat on the edge of the bed.

"I must really trust you, Nurse Raymond," she said with a weak laugh. "You could be giving me anything."

Her breath caught as she inhaled through the discomfort.

"Easy, Madame." The word slipped out without thought, catching us both off guard.

We shared a faint smile at the memory. Of me calling her Madame, of how easily I'd fallen back into the rhythm of pleasing her. Doing anything she asked... and a few things she hadn't even known she wanted.

I stepped into the bathroom to grab her a warm towel. When I returned, Ice was slowly repositioning herself against the tufted headboard, a pillow tucked protectively over her stomach. I handed her the towel, then sat beside her, watching.

She was beautiful. Even with the bonnet on and faint sleep lines tracing her smooth skin, she was still stunning. Her eyes looked brighter today, more rested. I was certain mine told a different story.

"You look like you have a lot on your mind, Mr. Raymond," she said, her hand drifting gently over the shell of my ear and down to my nape.

"Something like that," I murmured, tilting my head so my lips brushed against her fingers.

"Just in case you forgot, I'm a good listener," she teased.

I laughed, because she was. One of the best I'd ever known. A boisterous chuckle escaped me when she patted her lap, signaling for me to lie down. Something we used to do. I'd lay my head in her lap while she oiled my scalp and listened to me ramble about my wild dreams.

"I can't play in your locs anymore," she said, "but I guess the low cut will do." She winked and that shit was straight voodoo.

I laid my head against the pillow in her lap without hesitation. Her delicate strokes over my waves pulled my eyes closed. The silence between us wasn't awkward; it was necessary. We'd avoided this conversation long enough. I tried to start it in Bimini, but it was too soon.

Now, though... I believed she was ready. We were ready. Closing the past was the only way forward.

"I wanted you to be mine," I whispered.

The words were quiet, but they landed with a shrill boom, heavier than I'd intended for the start of this conversation.

Icelyn didn't respond, but her body went rigid. Her hand stilled. I reached up, covering it with mine, urging her not to stop. After a beat, she resumed her gentle strokes.

"I didn't want rented time anymore," I continued, my voice dropping. "No more secret weekends. I wanted you... completely. But my reality didn't align with yours. I didn't have shit to offer you. Not back then."

"Ray, that's not true," she said softly. "You... you were everything. I just wish you could've seen yourself the way I—"

"Don't," I interrupted, gentle but firm. "We both knew it wasn't sustainable. You had responsibilities. Kids. A whole life. And I was a college dropout juggling odd jobs, no plan, and a heart that didn't know how to beat without you in the room."

I exhaled shakily, pressing a kiss to her knee before lifting my gaze to hers.

"I'm a different man now, Icelyn. My heart still doesn't beat without you, but everything else has changed."

Her eyes glassed over. "Blaize—" she croaked, shaking her head.

If she'd been physically able, she would've bolted. Her gaze darted everywhere but at me. I cupped her chin, guiding her face back to mine. My eyes held hers—silent but insistent—urging her to talk to me.

"And now *my* shit is all fucked up," she cried, her shoulders lifting as her voice cracked. "I left my job and started a business with no clients. I miss my kids being in the house. And now this..." She gestured weakly to her body. "I'm empty, Blaize. Hollow."

I closed the distance like a starving man, like she was the last thing I'd ever touch. My breath came unsteady. Hers was worse. We were so close her tears might as well have been mine.

"Did you love me?" I asked, laying all my cards on the table. "Back then... did you love me, Icelyn?"

She immediately fell back into the position that made her feel safe. Like muscle memory, she buried her face against my chest, a silent sob rippling through her body. After a long heartbeat, I felt her head nod once... then again.

"Do you love me now?" I whispered into her ear, pressing a kiss to her temple.

We were both breathing too fast, the unsteady feeling making my stomach twist like I might vomit. She pulled back, trembling fingers wiping away the last of her tears.

After a deep inhale and a shaky exhale through swollen lips, she said, "Ray... Blaize... whatever your name is," followed by a soft, broken giggle. "I loved your young ass then... and I love you now."

My grin spread wide when I leaned in, kissing her slow and deliberate and desperate in the quiet way that mattered. Our tongues tangled as we held each other's gaze, neither of us willing to look away.

That Friday, all those years ago, was the night I lost her. The night *potential* wasn't enough. The night *love* wasn't enough.

But today, Icelyn Perry—my Madame Ice—was mine. No contracts. No temporary arrangements.

Just mine.

Forever.

## *icelyn*

"So you done had that in-home care dick, huh?" Sienna joked as she sipped from a long-stemmed wine glass.

It had been a couple of weeks since I'd seen my friend. She'd been busy hopping between travel excursions while I was home healing. Still, her adventures hadn't stopped her from thinking of me. The Uber Eats, grocery deliveries, and flowers were all greatly appreciated.

I shook my head, laughing. "Girl, shut up. That man has definitely been taking care of me, though."

I stirred the red sauce simmering on the stove, nibbling my bottom lip as I thought back over the past six weeks. If Blaize Raymond were a song, he'd be Maxwell's *Whenever, Wherever, Whatever*. That man had been making house calls every single day since the day we said *I love you*.

I thought his care routine was stellar years ago, but

grown-man—*my man, my man, my mutherfuckin' man*—had taken it to another level. Warm baths once I could finally submerge in water. Washing my hair. Massaging my scalp. Tending to every inch of my body like it was his prized possession.

We layed naked and talked for hours into the night. He told me about his ex-wife, Alyssa, and their daughter, Blyss. About how he'd thought about looking for me every day.

Once I was back on my feet, we started cooking dinner together and slow-dancing to our old playlist in the living room. It had been a long time since I'd felt loved like that. Hell, I hadn't been loved like that *since* Blaize.

"Girl, look at you," SiSi snickered. "Blushing and shit."

"You're crazy. Come on so I can try this outfit on," I said, heading toward my bedroom.

Minutes later, I stepped out of the closet in a crisp white, form-fitting mini dress trimmed with red piping and a matching cap. The fabric hugged my waist and hips with just enough stretch, the hemline resting just below the curve of my booty. The plunging neckline accentuated my some-what-perky double Ds, and the buttons down the front promised easy access later.

"Come on, Nurse Ice," SiSi quipped. "That boy is going to lose his mind when he sees you, sis."

"That's the plan," I sang. "Now skedaddle. He'll be here in less than an hour, and I still need to do my makeup," I said, shooing her away.

Today marked six weeks since my hospital discharge,

and I was officially cleared to return to all physical activities. *Including Blaize.*

He'd taken such good care of me that I wanted to do something special for him. Hence the nurse's costume, two bottles of Pinot Noir, and one of his favorite meals—seafood linguini with red sauce, garlic-cheese bread, and grilled zucchini.

Tonight, Madame Ice would be making her long-awaited return.

# *blaize*

I pulled into Ice's garage around seven o'clock. I'd finished my shift, picked up Blyss from school, then dropped her at a friend's house for a birthday sleepover. The girl had just started school and already had a packed social calendar.

I'd been looking forward to tonight with my lady. *Goddamn...* Icelyn mutherfucking Perry was mine. And the shit felt real... right. Since my daughter came back from spending the summer with her mom, we hadn't been able to be together every night like we had when Ice was healing.

But she and Blyss had become fast friends, even though they hadn't met in person yet. My FaceTime calls with Icelyn had quickly turned into *our* calls with Ms. Ice.

I shot Icelyn a text to let her know I was here, just like she instructed. The garage door rumbled open as I killed the engine. Walking through the entrance, I expected to see her pretty face, but all that greeted me was the bomb-ass scent of my favorite dish. Candles flickered on the kitchen table beside two wine glasses and a bottle of red. *What was this woman up to?*

"Ice," I called out, heading down the hall toward her bedroom.

"I'm in here," she answered.

I stepped into the room, dimly lit by only the lamp on the nightstand. The lavender scent that she loved sifted from the diffuser. The ceiling fan turned, chilling the already cold space just like Icelyn preferred. My eyes circled around because I still hadn't laid eyes on her.

"Ice, baby, what are you doing? I see you cooked for me," I said, smiling as I kicked off my shoes and dropped onto the small loveseat in her room. "That's right on time. I'm starving."

The bathroom door slowly crept open, and my mouth damn near fell off my face. My Ice stood there dressed in a nurse's costume that barely covered the red panties peeking from underneath.

Curvy, cocoa-brown legs stood out against the stark white material. The curls I was used to seeing had been straightened, a soft bangs sweeping across smoky eyes. Perky breasts stood at attention like they were greeting me personally. But it was those blood-red, sky-high heels that held my attention.

"You starving for me or food?" she asked, strolling slowly

across the room with her bottom lip caught between her teeth.

"Fuucckk." That was all I could manage.

My dick was hard as a rock. I adjusted myself, trying to ease the pressure building in my pants. But damn, that good-smelling food would have to wait. It had been six weeks since she was back in my arms. But even longer since we'd been intimate in Bimini.

I needed to fuck her right the fuck now.

"You like?" she sang, stepping between my wide-open legs.

"I love," I shot back. "Damn, Ice. You look good as hell, baby."

"It's Madame Ice to you," she said with a lustful smirk.

I snickered because those words hit me like déjà vu. I buried my face against her stomach, sliding my hands up the backs of her thighs until I reached her ass. The red lace underneath was a welcome sight.

She knew I loved lace on her. And this ensemble did not disappoint.

"Remember when you told me to always tell you want I want. 'Don't sugarcoat shit with me, Ice'." The last sentence mocking me.

I laughed, nodding. "Tell me what you want, Madame Ice."

Her eyes scanned from my lazy ones down my chest, my stomach then my dick.

"I want that..." she pointed to my erection, "in my mouth."

I didn't have to tell her to say less, my actions spoke louder than any words could. Without breaking our stare, I pulled down my sweatpants and boxers at the same time. My dick shot straight up, springing free like it had been trapped in a cage too long.

Icelyn slowly lowered into a squat, and I couldn't help but be impressed by her balance in those sky-high heels. I didn't know if it was the way her eyes dipped low or how her tongue grazed her lips, but something about her told me she was hungry... for me.

She leaned in, brushing a kiss across the tip of my dick that sent a sharp jolt through me. Pulling back, she wore a satisfied smile like she already knew what she was about to do. She opened her mouth then slid her tongue over the head. Ice didn't rush. She never did. Her movements were slow but not lazy... deliberate.... focused. And damn... she was thorough.

Icelyn was a savage when twisting, turning, and sucking in a cadence that had my head tipping back, my body giving in piece by piece until it was just me and her in that moment.

"Madame... fuck, baby," I groaned, my voice breaking under the pressure building inside me.

She didn't let up. Didn't slow down. If anything, she leaned into it, unrelenting, confident, and in complete control of the rhythm she'd set. Her mouth suctioned around me, then wiggled her tongue like she was sucking on a lolipop while caressing my balls.

I fucking lost it.

My hand slid into her hair, not to stop her, but to guide

her. But she didn't need any help. Her pace was flawless. Fucking impeccable.

"Damn, Ma... shit," I grunted, my breath uneven.

"Mmmhmm," she hummed, pleased with her performance.

"Madame Ice... Icelyn... baby, I'm—"

My words fell apart, my breathing heavy, body tightening as everything came to a head but that didn't stop me from pumping in and out and in and out of her warm mouth.

For a split second, I thought about stopping her. Pulling her up so I could catch my breath. But then I remembered who I was dealing with. This wasn't the polished, put-together Icelyn Perry. This was my mutherfuckin' Madame Ice.

And she handled me completely without flinching. Just took everything I gave her... every single drop.

Icelyn climbed on top of me. Straddling me right there on the couch. If this was where she wanted it, this was where I would deliver. I never not delivered for her.

Once by one, I popped every snap on her dress, revealing the matching red lace bra. Blackberry nipples distended against the dainty fabric. It appeared they wanted me just as much as I wanted them.

Unhooking her bra, I kept my eyes fixed on her beautiful face. Ice wanted to kiss me. She loved kissing me. But I wouldn't allow it. Not yet. While Madame Ice always thought she was in control, I ran this shit. And right now, I wanted her breasts against my lips. One by one, I licked, then sucked and licked then sucked.

"Ray. Kiss me," she demanded through a moan.

I chuckled because usually that command would be my pleasure, but I wanted her closer to the edge before I granted her my lips.

"Uh-uh. Not yet," I teased, dodging her attempt.

Her mouth found the curve of my neck, her labored breaths warm against my skin. I shook my head because Icelyn's hardheaded ass was relentless. Between every lick and soft peck, she inhaled my scent like it offered momentary satisfaction until she got what she wanted. But the languid pace of her rhythm had me ready to concede.

Roughly, I gripped the back of her neck and shifted her to face me, forcing our eyes to connect. There was nothing random about the way I examined her. Nothing accidental about the intention, or the intensity behind my gaze.

For a second, she stilled beneath my hand, her breathing uneven, those stubborn eyes searching mine like she was daring me to look away first. I didn't.

I'd enjoyed the time we'd spent together over the past several weeks because it hadn't been about sex. It was about connection... *reconnection*. Getting reacquainted. Peeling back the layers time had placed between us and discovering who she had become and who we still were to each other.

But I missed our physical joining. Missed the warmth and softness of my manhood wrapped in her essence.

Damn, I didn't want to succumb to those pleading eyes. But I did. I kissed her. As hungry as I was to feel her, it was tender and unrushed. Ice's pointy nails drifted up my nape before clutching the back of my head, deepening the kiss.

Then deeper. She knew she'd won. Shit, I didn't care. I'd yield to her every fucking time.

She lifted slightly to grip me with one hand. My dick had no issue coming back to life. Not with this woman rocking her lace-covered pussy over my steel. Icelyn didn't want gentle passion. She wanted to be fucked. So I obliged.

Well, *she* obliged. Guided me between her slick folds before allowing me dive deeper and deeper until I was drowning. The flesh of her fat ass unhurriedly pounded onto my thighs.

Rise to the tip, circle, circle, slide.

Rise to the tip, circle, circle, slide.

At this pace, I was about to be a one-minute man. I couldn't do shit but lay back and take it. I was familiar with every bend and swell of her beautiful body but watching her work my dick like a damn vixen was like watching my favorite movie on repeat.

"Goddamn, Ice. Shit," I groaned.

Her fleshy center wrapped around me like silk over stone. My Madame Ice had the thickest thigh's I'd ever seen and she tightened them shits around my waist with every roll and bounce. Our heads fell back in unison, mouths hanging open, desperate to find air. No words or sounds were needed to know that we were falling without a parachute. No gravity, no way out, just endless depth.

"Mmhmm," she moaned, nibbling her bottom lip vainly attempting to quell her smile. Her lips brushed the shell of my ear before whispering, "Let it go, Blaize. You deserve this, baby." She caught my earlobe between her teeth with a bite that wasn't meant to be gentle.

"Fuck, Ice," I breathed, the sound rougher than I intended.

"Uh-uh. Say my name," she said, a hint of aggression sharpening her tone.

I stayed quiet. Not because I didn't want to answer. My ass couldn't answer. The moment was stretching higher with every sway of her hips, the pressure building toward an electrifying climax that was stealing the words right out of me.

"Tell me... Fire," she whispered.

My eyes lifted the second she said it. That name. Her name for me.

She was stunning, riding me slow, sweat-damp strands of hair clinging to her temple while she watched me like she knew exactly what she was doing to me.

"Mada..." I tried.

Ice settled onto me, clamping down every time I tried to speak. This goddamn woman was fucking with me.

"Madame..." I managed. "Ma...Madame Ice," I damn near shouted.

I collapsed back on the couch, pulling her with me so she rested against my chest. We didn't speak. We didn't have to. Lazily, I traced my fingertips up and down her spine while our breathing slowed. Her body felt heavy against mine, exhausted in a way that came from letting go completely.

After a moment, she lifted herself just enough to look at

me. A soft smile curved across her lips before she leaned down and pressed a sweet kiss to mine.

"Thank you," she murmured.

"For what?" I rasped.

A quiet moment passed between us before she whispered, "Everything."

*icelyn*

Twelve years seemed like yesterday every time Blaize touched me. He touched me like he'd studied my body, spoke to me like he'd researched my soul. This man had me in ways I refused to admit out loud. And now here we were, half-naked in my bed after eating our weight in seafood pasta and wine, simply enjoying each other.

Yes, we both gained years and maybe a little wisdom, but the gravitational pull between us—the undeniable attraction, that same fire, hadn't cooled one damn degree. Because no matter how much I tried to deny fate, defy what the universe was leading me towards, Blaize and I were still dangerous for each other.

Lethal in a way that scared me. Not because he'd hurt me, but because of how deeply I knew he could matter to me. Shit, how much he *did* matter to me.

"Get out of your head, Icelyn Perry." The bass in his voice was rough. He sounded half-asleep, his head resting in my lap as my hand stroked through his thick hair.

"Whatever do you mean, Mr. Raymond?" I said playful but irritated that he could sense my angst even without seeing my face.

"Your stroke is heavy, out of rhythm. That's how I know you've got a lot on your mind."

He sprinkled soft kisses along my knee, the tip of his nose brushing gently against my skin.

"Hmm," I hummed to give myself a little time to process my sporadic thoughts.

Blaize remained quiet, understanding my need for time to gather my thoughts.

"This is scary," I finally said after several moments ticked by.

"This?" he said questioningly.

I nodded as if he could see me. "Yes. This. Whatever *this* is," I scoffed.

He unhurriedly flipped over with the back of his head pressed against my legs. I shrugged, pursing me lips when he looked at me.

"Everything doesn't have to be defined, Ice," he said, mimicking my shoulder shrug. "How we started was spontaneous and crazy and undefined. Every weekend we were together, we created what we wanted it to be. We didn't need a title or definition. It was just *us*... I'm your fire and you're my ice."

Blaize released a lazy exhale as his eyes lowered. "No

pressure to be anything other than what we want to be," he said slowly, waving a finger between the two of us.

Sleep settled over him then, soft and insistent, like he was already drifting through a good dream. "Whether it's for a moment or a lifetime," he murmured, his words slurred with exhaustion, "I just want to love you."

And with that, the sandman finally swept him away.

## *sisi*

A FEW MONTHS LATER....

Bryson's twenty-fifth birthday in Vegas was easily one of my best-curated experiences. And trust me, I'd curated some damn good ones.

Leave it to my godson to plan a full weekend with his crew in the city that never slept and insisted that his mama be there for every second of it. That was the thing about Ice and her kids; they were not just family, they were a unit. A crew. Bryson might be grown now, but that boy was still his mama's baby.

So when he said Vegas, Auntie SiSi made sure Vegas showed up properly. Penthouse suites. VIP tables. Poolside day parties. And tonight's grand gathering at Nobu to kick off the weekend.

Everybody was there. Including my best friend's fine-ass, dark-chocolate man, Blaize.

I leaned against the host stand, holding a fancy champagne flute, watching the entrance like I was waiting for the opening scene of a movie. Because I didn't want to miss a minute of this must-see main event. I knew the history between Icelyn and Blaize better than anybody, so tonight was about to be something.

My girl hadn't brought a man around her family since she and Sonny split for good. So the fact that Blaize accompanied her to Vegas? Huge. Big. Ginormous step.

Ever since my friend came to her senses and locked that man down, they'd been inseparable. Still wrapped up in their little love bubble, but tonight, she finally let that man out in the wild for the world to see.

And here he was in Vegas. Meeting... *everybody.*

Bryson and Kamryn were standing near the entrance talking to their dad, Sonny, and his long-time goofy girlfriend while the rest of the group filtered in. Then the elevator dinged and the doors slid open. And I nearly laughed into my champagne because *bay-bee...* Icelyn Perry knew how to make an entrance.

Black faux-leather leggings hugged those thick thighs like a second skin. An off-the-shoulder asymmetrical sweater showing just enough skin to remind the room she was still *that* girl. Studded Saint Laurent boots that said she wasn't nobody's quiet little mama.

But the real showstopper? The broad, bearded man holding her hand.

Blaize Raymond walked beside Ice like a bodyguard with

benefits. Kevin Costner energy, protecting every curve and dip of her body. He made simple dark gray distressed jeans, a black Lacoste sweater, and all-black Gucci sneakers look way more complicated than they had any business being.

Half the women in the lobby paused, looking from him... then to their men like they were reconsidering their life choices.

And the way he held Ice's hand, softly brushing his thumb across her skin? Yeah...That shit wasn't casual. Every head turned as they walked through the lobby. I took a slow sip and smiled to myself. *Oh, this about to be good.*

Bryson spotted them first, his face wearing the same rich skin tone as his mother's, already dipped in a scowl.

"Happy birthday, baby boy," Icelyn said, wrapping him in a hug.

"Hey, Ma," he answered, though his eyes were already sliding past her toward the tall man standing beside her.

Kamryn stepped in for her hug next, a new boo hovering proudly at her side. Thankfully, she finally kicked David's broke ass back to the streets where he belonged. My Godbaby was glowing these days, smiling every time the caramel-skinned cutie whispered something sweet in her ear.

This was Kam's first official meeting with Blaize, aside from the brief introduction they'd had while Icelyn was recovering. It had finally clicked why he looked so familiar. He was the man her mom always said saved her life. What Kam didn't realize, though, was just how close her mother had been to that life-saving stranger all those years ago.

After embracing her daughter, Icelyn turned to greet Bryson Sr. "Hi, Sonny."

His eyes roamed over the mother of his children, looking a little too intrigued by Ice's bodacious frame, considering his girlfriend was standing right beside him.

"Hey...Icelyn," he replied. But his attention had already shifted. Right to Blaize.

I pressed my lips together to keep from laughing because the tension was thick. As long as I could remember, Icelyn had two protectors—her son and her baby daddy.

Bryson folded his arms. Sonny tilted his head. Both of them looked Blaize up and down like they were assessing a situation that hadn't been cleared through proper channels.

Then, almost at the same time, they asked, "Who is this?"

I nearly choked on the bubbly tickling my throat.

Ice didn't answer right away. Instead, she turned toward Blaize. And before anybody in that lobby could prepare themselves for what was about to happen, she kissed him. Not a polite little introduction kiss. No ma'am. That kiss said *my man, my man, my man.* Or better yet, *my dick, my dick, my dick.* She was finally claiming him the way she was always meant to. *About damn time.*

When Ice pulled back, she looked between her son, her daughter, and Sonny like nothing about that moment required explanation.

"This..." she said, smiling as she traced her fingers tenderly down Blaize's cheek. "...is Blaize."

She paused just long enough for the room to hang on her next words.

"My fire."

**The End**

# author's note

Well, well, well... What can I say about Blaize and Icelyn? Fire, right?

I truly enjoyed every minute of writing this sexy, sultry romance about a woman in her forties who hasn't lost her spark. If anything, she reignited the flame. And having Blaize as her fire? Whew... that didn't hurt one bit.

That fine, young tenda was absolutely everything. Not just in the way he adored her body but in the way he showed up for her mind, her heart, and her healing.

Their story is about more than chemistry. It's about timing, growth, and what happens when two people meet again as the versions of themselves they were always meant to become.

Now tell me... what did you think about Fire & Ice?

If you loved Blaize and Icelyn (or even if they got on your

nerves a little ✶✶ ), I'd love for you to leave a review on Amazon and wherever books are sold.

And before you go…I've got something special for you.

**You're officially invited to the Love Notes Lounge**

This is my private reader space where we go beyond the pages. Inside the Lounge, we talk about the books, the characters, the moments that had you clutching your chest (or your pearls ☺ ), and everything in between. You'll get behind-the-scenes content, exclusive sneak peeks, bonus scenes, and a closer connection to me and the stories you love.

Scan the code and join us for free or step into one of the VIP experiences for even more access.

I'll be waiting for you in the Lounge. 💋

*With Love,*
*Robbi Renee*

9 781954 767515